RahGor Motivations & Publishing

Unfinished Projects © 2013
by Sheryl Felecia Means

Edited by Robert H. Hastings

ISBN # 978-0-9889954-0-6

Manufactured in the United States of America.

Cover Design: Sheryl Felecia Means
Interior Formatting: Eclipse Graffix

RahGor Motivations
45 Rockefeller Plaza
630 Fifth Avenue, 20th Floor
New York, NY 10111
(646) 358-4966 -office
(646) 358-4878- fax
info@rahgor.com

Unfinished Projects
A Novel by Sheryl Felecia Means

Prologue

The old man was lying in the hospital bed, half dead and incoherent, not sure of how many days he'd been there or how long he had to live.

Doctors continually visited his hospital room, poking and prodding; nurses followed, taking vial after vial of blood, inserting another IV, and then injecting medicines – anything to keep him alive and awake, albeit temporarily.

Thick tears rolled down his cheeks. He was painfully aware that he would die soon.

The police found him at home on the metal table he used to build chairs, tables, and other furniture. He received the table as a gift – a replacement for the wooden one he crafted for himself after leaving the army. His baby – the youngest of his daughters and his favorite child – wanted the table he made for herself. "I will finally have a family heirloom!" she exclaimed, though secretly, she was mostly excited about the prospect of having a piece of home in her apartment.

He remembered letting her join him in building things shortly after her mother died. She was extremely angry as a child, and he hoped to help her channel her frustrations by way of a hammer and saw. He did the same out of grief for his dearly beloved, and he hoped they would get through it together.

Where is my baby girl, now?

The procedure he underwent on the table was brutal – no anesthetics and a metal device held his tongue in place to stifle his screams. He was barely breathing when he was found, and he was badly bruised.

"Your vocal chords and tonsils have been removed, sir." Even the doctor was mortified. No voice. He would be unable to speak ever again.

You're nothing but an old dog and a coward!

The tears were falling heavier now, eroding canals and asymmetric pathways of self-pity, fear, and regret.

Whoever did this to him didn't take anything from the house. Everything was in its order with the exception of a few slashed and broken pictures of his baby girl. The old man was brutalized; several ribs were broken along with his fingers, and he was bleeding internally. He'd never been a fighting man, but he always defended himself. However, last night was different; he didn't have control. Some rowdy group had jumped him, he recalled; at least, he surmised there were multiple people. Someone had sneaked upon him at his own house.

Small clues to the situation arrived and escaped his memory as he expired on the hard bed. He wished he had a pen. Then, he recalled that all of his

UNFINISHED PROJECTS

fingers were broken with his own mallet. He figured he wouldn't live long enough to write anything.

The tears were now uncontrollable.

The police were searching for clues from anyone who could explain why someone would want to hurt the old man and for someone who might have seen what happened. Every now and then, the young officer who found him – a man the age of his eldest daughter and someone his wife had taught as a boy – visited him and just talked. It was a small town, and everyone knew everything. For the first time, the old man was grateful for that.

"People noticed your car hadn't moved from its spot all morning and got worried. Mrs. J. from across the street called me and told me your door was open and that someone should come see about you. I'm glad I did, sir."

Calling him "sir" was a formality the young man couldn't wait to take advantage of, and he smiled as he said it. The irony was not lost on the old man – after all, he hadn't worn a uniform since he worked as an army technician, and he never demanded or wanted that kind of respect. However, his tired, battered, and weak grin didn't last long before the tears were streaming again, etching their way down his ashen face. The young man retrieved a tissue and slowly wiped as many tears as he could, but they constantly flowed. Soon, he felt a wet line form along his own cheek.

"I'm sorry," the young man whispered, wiping the stray tear from his face with the back of his hand.

The old man slowly shook his head and gingerly lifted his arm in dismissal, the effort visibly exhausting him. He was barely holding on.

"Don't worry, Mr. Woods," he muttered half-heartedly. "We'll find one of your daughters soon."

Chapter 1

It was 8:30 in the morning when Anthony awakened on Friday, a day he typically reserved for alternately watching cartoons and the news.

Why on earth would Jones agree to a Friday morning meeting?

He didn't bother to get coffee because he was already late. In fact, he should have been leaving the house when he woke up. After he showered and cleaned the lines on his growing scruff of a beard, he hastily ate a granola bar. He was still in a towel, moving at a glacial pace, and when it was eight fifty-five, the inevitable happened.

"Where you at white boy?"

"Jones, I'm blacker than you."

With heavy laughter and the same quip, Jones responded, "Have you looked in a mirror lately?"

It was a routine. They'd developed it after a lifetime of knowing one another, growing up in the same town, and being what some would call best friends. In reality, they were more like brothers. Anthony and Jones fought frequently. At the end of a physical fight, when some temporary truce was made, they'd end up brushing off one another, grinning mischievously. "Your momma is gonna kill you for ripping up that new shirt." "Me? That was all you, and I intend to tell her so, too. She'll find you and tear into your hide."

UNFINISHED PROJECTS

They grew up in one of those towns in the South that was frozen in the past with Confederate flags, cotton fields, cows, and parks named after segregationist generals. Jones' mother, Mrs. Brown, was still cleaning houses for affluent families in town as her mother had, and Anthony's family was one of them. He could honestly say that Mrs. Brown was the one person his mother truly respected. Anthony's mother, Mrs. James, and Mrs. Brown attended the same elementary school and graduated together from high school. When Mrs. Brown first married, she and Mrs. James went shopping together. This was the model Anthony grew up with, learning to respect all of his elders – black, white, and yellow because it was the right thing to do.

Accompanied by Jones, Anthony drove to meet with Jeffries. Entering the building and right before stepping into Jeffries' office, he saw a beautiful woman dash past him carrying food. Because of his early lessons to respect all persons equally, he wasn't surprised this African-American woman invaded his senses.

Anthony could have sworn he heard her cuss under her breath. *Did she just say shit?* He stopped himself from protesting about how ladies shouldn't swear, since it seemed appropriate for a gamine like her. He counted as she ran back and forth past Jeffries' door three more times.

UNFINISHED PROJECTS

Anthony allowed his long legs to stretch out lazily, checking for the small ping of the elevator, and ignoring the conversation Jones and Jeffries were having. *Jones and Jeffries*, he mused. *Now that's a partnership.* It was true that he didn't possess much in the way of business savvy and could honestly say he didn't want to; he was much more interested in production. Yet, he owned seventy-five percent of the controlling interest of Jeffries' company, a group that produced reasonably priced metals for plane parts and other products. He reasoned early that he couldn't leave his 'brother' to his own devices with the money Mrs. Brown left, for Jones would have spent it all.

Anthony stretched his legs again, feeling a pull all the way in his toes and thought about the day that would come when he could go into early retirement with someone like the woman running frantically just outside the door.

"White boy." He was rudely reminded of the present.

Why do you insist upon calling me that in public?

"Yeah, Jones?"

"You call him 'white boy'? And you haven't been lynched? That's a laugh!" Jeffries said as his voice echoed around the office, his chins shaking, and his disingenuous smile widening. He looked like a black Santa, almost pink in the cheeks and choking on his own insincerity. Jones laughed with him.

UNFINISHED PROJECTS

Anthony simply grinned nervously, shrugged it off, and ventured to answer a question he hadn't heard. He was distracted. He wanted to go and help that beautiful woman set up all that food and demand an explanation as to why she'd assaulted his senses with her presence.

She'd look at him and giggle, eyes batting like a mischievous and enchanting creature. He imagined her kissing him on the nose or the cheek – some place innocent as a good girl would do, but then she'd breathe in his ear before giving him an answer and send him reeling again.

"Let's get out of this office, Jeffries. I don't want him lost in his head again," Jones said.

Suddenly, they were in the meeting with everyone vying for power. The environment was overwhelming, but when she came in, Anthony swore he smelled her perfume from across the gap of middle-aged business men and women, wrapped up in the tangle of their industry, prematurely gray, and more in love with their careers than those who wore the match to the gold and silver bands on their left ring fingers.

Don't look at her and you won't do anything stupid, he reasoned with himself. *Just be cool and when she leaves, it won't matter*. He looked anxiously around him, at his phone, and the wall – anywhere but those pretty brown eyes.

"Order, man. I'm hungry."

UNFINISHED PROJECTS

Yes and she's not a steak. Several people anxiously turned their attention to him. Why hadn't he said anything? *They'd find you odd. You've barely contributed to this meeting, and now you want to play superhero and defend Jeffries' assistant from the other side of the room.* He shook it off, increasingly aware of her eyes on him. He hoped he wasn't red.

"I'll have the same thing he's having."

The woman left the room too quickly. *Did I say that dismissively?* Right before she left was there a hint of disappointment, or was he imagining things? She'd looked at him in an amusing way; of that he was certain. He couldn't defend himself, not in front of everyone. *Leave a card,* he thought. *Have her call.* He knew she wouldn't call. His mother would be angry with him for such an expectation.

He barely walked in the door that evening before visiting Jeffries' company website to try and locate a number to reach her. "All urgent matters may be handled by my assistant at the number below." *Wow, the lazy jerk didn't even have the courtesy to post his number.* He was glad for Jeffries' laziness in that moment. *Yes, this is an urgent matter, indeed.* He dialed the number.

"Hello" – she sounded as if she was singing to him – "this is the voicemail of...." *Damn.*

Less than fifteen minutes later, "Hi, um, someone called me from this number earlier? Is this is an emergency for J. Parts, Incorporated?" She sounded

13

annoyed. It was a little before six o'clock in the evening.

"Are you asking me or telling me?" His mother's words bounced off the walls and back into him. They were out before he could stop himself.

"I guess that's something you'll have to figure out some other time." There was a change in her tone; she was semi-sweet now, and he knew it had something to do with his voice. He previously had used his voice to his advantage.

"Quick and beautiful, I like that." *You're inescapably corny.*

Then emerged the sweetest sound he'd ever heard. She was giggling, a sound like milk and honey, sugar rolling off her tongue and feeding the masses.

"Who is this?" She was still giggling, and he felt himself melting into the floor.

"My name is Anthony."

"Hello, Anthony," the smile still in her voice. "My name is Felicity."

"That's a beautiful name," he responded as he allowed his drawl to emerge. He was truly a Mississippian at heart. He couldn't place where she was from.

"If you're always this nice, I might let you call me more than once."

His blood rose. *Gamine.*

UNFINISHED PROJECTS

"You shouldn't speak that way, miss. It's bad for my health."

Then, she giggled again. He decided he'd chuckle with her; he liked the sound of their voices mingling on the phone. By the time they had finished talking, it was nine o'clock.

Chapter 2

He's white.

Unfortunately, after meeting Anthony at Del Frisco's and being seated, it's the only thing Felicity noticed about him; whether or not she disliked it would be determined later. They'd only spoken on the phone twice before in the two weeks since what she assumed was their first encounter, and race wasn't a topic during their conversations. He had this deep-toned voice, syrupy and thick – it'd be pulled taffy if it were candy or caramel and melted chocolate. Her father spoke the same way, slowly and thickly, every syllable deepening his meaning and his intentions; she supposed that was the reason she was disappointed.

This boy is a far cry from Daddy.

Felicity felt her shoulders release, and she recognized for the first time that she was tense. It wasn't nervousness that had her biting her lip or her fingernail or anything she put near her mouth as much as it was anticipation that she wouldn't like him and that he wouldn't like her. She allowed a small bit of disappointment to register on her face as they sat down, testing the waters. She wanted her face to read, "Go home, honky," but in spite of herself, she ended up grinning like a sweetheart and making an earnest attempt at a good time.

Now, she took note of his clothing, finding him finely dressed from top to bottom, somehow rugged and dapper. He wore a gray button-up shirt which he left hanging haphazardly over the top of his dark-washed jeans that had a certain edge to them. She recognized the shoes immediately – her father was an enthusiast when it came to good church clothes – and she smirked at the black Ferragamos, the corner of her mouth turning upward in appreciation.

Suddenly, she was aware that she was staring and became self-conscious, her short and curly Afro burdensome somehow, the wooden earrings shaped like Africa swinging slightly in her ears, offensive. She acknowledged her African gesture as pretentious; not every brother was down for the motherland, and in truth, she wasn't either. She never left the American South for longer than a weekend.

"Have you recently read about the conflict going on in central Africa?"

He's been talking to you this whole time, and you've been sizing him up, idiot. Say something. She'd forgotten they were supposed to be in conversation at all, and his voice, that sweet voice, made all the more enigmatic by the nature of its owner, brought her back to earth.

"I'm going to be honest with you. I haven't been paying much attention at all." She released a nervous laugh and awkwardly wrung her hands.

17

Even she didn't know what she was commenting on, her inattentiveness to the past two minutes of his one-sided conversation or the conflict in Africa. He smiled at her and regarded her closely, his head tilted and his eyes squinted. She was glad that he was staring, too, happy for the change of pace; it seemed to her as if the world was in conflict. She didn't want to talk about that now – she wanted comfort.

"No, you've been trying to get a read from me." She was taken aback that he was that discerning. As a matter of fact, she was intrigued that he was discerning at all. He had her attention. "It's in your body language, the shift of your eyes. You're very subtle about it. Congrats."

Okay, smart ass, she thought to herself as she smirked, lifting her glass to take a sip of water.

"Don't insult me in your mind when I'm not up there to defend myself."

Felicity almost choked and dropped the glass. Anthony definitely had her attention.

Felicity's sister said she needed a man, and she didn't believe it until she found the card on her desk. In spite of being ignorant to which of the two men it belonged, she felt apprehensions. The Tyrant, a term of endearment she used for her employer and business tycoon, Mr. Jeffries, had been in a meeting with the owner of the business card and several others during an extended lunch. The Tyrant requested she bring in breakfast at eight o'clock that morning – "nothing special, just Starbucks" which proved to her wallet and gas mileage to be very special, indeed – and by one o'clock, the room wanted lunch, as well.

She walked with caution into the most spacious meeting room in the office. She had been summoned in light of the second assistant's mysterious absence so, like a 'good girl,' she stepped quietly through the door.

"Yes, Mr. Jeffries?" She hated the way she sounded, this cross between too-shy-for-her-own-good and we-are-having-an-affair-behind-your-wife's-back, an echo of everything she detested about the assumptions implicit with her job description.

Six sets of eyes were on her when she walked into the room, and none were female. Surprisingly and disappointingly, one man had his head down. The rest trained their glances to her legs. She acknowledged them as her defining feature, along with her smile and the way her nose scrunched when she laughed.

Most people didn't expect her to be as tall as five feet, six inches, dwarfed behind her monstrous desk and shrouded by ever increasing stacks of paperwork. But to many men, she was still tiny. *Don't objectify me you pigs. Have you married men no shame at all?* She was thinking all the right things – things she'd never say for the sake of keeping her job, but in a dark cavern in her mind, she liked that they were looking.

Her grandmother used to say that she'd die an old maid – "too many curves, big legs, and a big mouth." Yet, here she stood at the center of all this male attention. Her brow furrowed as she noticed him actively working to look away from her. Why wouldn't that white man look at her the way all the other men were? She shrugged it off. *Gay*, she sighed. *Too bad.*

Two weeks later and he was sitting in front of her, willing to pay for dinner and reading her like a book.

"You're thinking and not talking," Anthony continued after Felicity stared at him blankly.

"You have no idea what I'm thinking, though. Do you believe that suggestive facial expressions are enough evidence to make conclusions about my thoughts?"

"Do you talk in circles to avoid the crux of the conversation?" Anthony asked.

"Which is?"

"That I make you uncomfortable. Because you thought the card I left on your desk belonged to my partner. Because you thought I was a black man when we talked on the phone."

Knowingly – that's how he looked at her, and it made her squirm within herself. *He shouldn't be allowed to see all that.* She felt naked and vulnerable before him, splayed open to be analyzed. So many truths were spat back at her in less than three minutes, but it wasn't venomous in nature. He was genuinely curious and behaved as though he wanted to prove to her that maybe she wasn't the only one who thought past her nose and that maybe he could keep up.

At the prompting of her employer, the Tyrant, everyone began loudly ordering food from Daily Grill, a well-liked restaurant in the mall. *Half-way across fucking town.* She'd have to call ahead, but there would still be a wait. The white mystery man hadn't barked orders at her like everyone else, including the women. However, his partner, a tall black man who was built like a basketball player and overly loud, gave him a sideways pat on the shoulder. "Order, man. I'm hungry," he said as he stole another glance back at her legs.

"I'll have the same thing he's having," he muttered.

With a slight frown, she scribbled the note on her pad, nodded, and left quickly. His awkward silence, instead of putting her at ease, made her more uncomfortable than before. *Why wouldn't he look at me?*

Felicity returned with the food to find that not only had the mystery man and his partner left the meeting – *and me with extra food* – but that one of them left a card on her desk with a cell phone number scribbled on the back. The secretary who vanished earlier now reappeared and said that a man left the message that he awaited her phone call.

"What'd he look like?"

"I don't know, black suit."

Thanks a lot.

"I didn't call you because I thought it was your partner…" Felicity started to say. *Was that entirely true? Should I tell him that they both made me uncomfortable? No.*

"Say what you're thinking, please." Anthony looked nervous and started twiddling his thumbs.

He's genuinely into you so, please, just say it. Out it went.

"I found your partner obnoxious at the very least, and I thought of you as odd. I didn't like the fact that you weren't looking at me like all the other men in the room because I wasn't sure what that meant. I didn't exactly enjoy that they were looking at me either, but I'm used to the same reaction from everyone, the constants. You were the variable in the situation. I felt how I feel now…." Her voice trailed off.

"Anxious," he nodded, sage-like and understanding.

"Yeah," she breathed. It felt like more of a release than the situation warranted, but she was glad it was finally out. "I'm just anxious."

"Do you know why?" Anthony asked. For the first time that night, he looked as though he didn't know either.

"No," Felicity breathed, "No, I don't."

Chapter 3

She thinks I like getting these calls from her in the middle of the night. She's wasting my time, and I have my own life. I don't want to hear from her anymore, and I should make that clear. One day I will stop answering the phone for her; I will just hit ignore or let it ring. She won't like it, and I won't care. Ha. She met someone. No one is going to love her like me, though. He makes her feel more than she wants to about him. It serves her right since she left me numb.

Jonathan brooded in his empty apartment with the lights off and the smoke of cigarettes and cigars making the space even smaller. The thick aroma choked him in his misplaced misery.

"I don't know what to think of him, Johnny. I never liked anybody like this except maybe you once. Do you think it's too soon to care about somebody?"

"No. It's never too soon." *After all, I cared about you from day one. I still care.*

Felicity sighed on the other line. *I remember what that sigh would feel like on my neck.* One involuntary movement and he found himself running his fingers over the very spot, now over grown by a beard he hadn't bothered to shave.

"So he's white?" His mouth spoke before he could stop it.

Felicity sighed again, and Johnny knew that this sigh meant she was frustrated. *No, please don't be angry with me.*

"I just wanted to ask my closest friend's opinion of a guy and my feelings, and you're thinking about race. You're so childish. I don't understand why that's relevant to our conversation, light as you are."

Jonathan couldn't get a grip on his anger, which was rising every second. He hated arguing with Felicity because he wanted her back in a dangerous way. He wanted her in a way even he didn't understand, more to have and hold than to love and cherish. Now she was focused on his little comment, and he wouldn't be able to turn the conversation around.

"You don't get what I'm saying, do you? You don't see the progression? You have been dating guys that are lighter and whiter. You started with me."

Felicity groaned out of resignation or disinterest; he couldn't tell. Silence and tension were building. Unknowingly, he'd made reference to his own color complex and insecurities. He had overstepped his boundaries. *She overstepped her fucking boundaries. I don't want to talk to her. Why did I even pick up the phone?*

"Thanks for listening, Johnny boy." Her tone was bitter now.

"Anytime."

25

UNFINISHED PROJECTS

Don't call me again. I'm begging you.
"Later."
Earlier, she sounded so happy, but it wasn't meant to last; their conversations always ended on a sour note.
"Yeah. Later."

Chapter 4

The bed was soft – too soft. She was not in her apartment.

Damn it, Felicity.

This was the ugly cycle that she wanted so desperately to break, the same way she tried to get off prescription medicines. Yet, there was a rush of uncertainty and danger that she couldn't describe. *Danger.*

"It's not as if I plan to jump your bones or something, Miss Lady," Anthony said. "I'm not a stalker."

"I know that," she nodded, allowing a small smile to reach her lips before biting it back nervously. "I just don't like the butterflies I'm fighting down. You make me somewhat nervous."

Anthony smiled.

Felicity found it odd that this part of their conversation brought her back to a night at yet another stranger's house, her last day with Jonathan.

"Hey, you all right, Felicity?" *Oh, no. It must be on my face.*

She told him she was fine, excused herself, and said that he could order for her if the waitress ever came back. *She's taking a really long time.*

Anthony smiled and said that he didn't know what she wanted.

"Surprise me," Felicity said as she winked. Ironically, he already had in a way by being white and also by staying and talking with her while she drifted in and out of reverie.

In the bathroom, Felicity stared at herself in thought, adjusting her make-up arbitrarily so she wouldn't look odd and switching out her African earrings for pearls. *This will be another test for you, white boy, to see if you're paying attention.* She examined her curves and her hair in the mirror. *I should probably grow this out.* She then looked at her skin; she was black but not as dark brown as her sisters, aptly named Ebony and Mahogany. They were the type of black that could be seen and tasted, undeniably of African descent. They were black like her mother.

Still, her skin was what attracted Jonathan to her.

Jonathan was barely black. When they met in high school, Felicity thought he would try to pass for white, which wouldn't take much effort on his part. She knew without a doubt he was black, but none of the white kids seemed to recognize him as such. "That's why I love you," he'd say, "because you see me." It must have hurt him to have his identity go unacknowledged that way for years – to know that he was black, a thing that his mob of unknowing white friends would happily deny. She suddenly felt a pang. *No. No sympathy for him, remember? That's why we're here - for break up sex.*

Whoever he was or to whomever he belonged would be resolved later, if he ever called. He probably wouldn't. She had a term paper due, and she knew that Jonathan would be waiting at her apartment to go to the library with her whether they'd argued or not. It was a quality about him that made her stomach churn – that he got to be inherently good and sweet and that she couldn't help being a careless brute, one not intentionally created or expected but there to deal with all the same.

Every one of her actions took on a tornado's qualities, especially after an argument. Jonathan's heated passion met with her cool indifference over something small – the way she'd look at another guy or ignored him – and they would crash into one another, words building uncontrollable wind tunnels around them that dug up the past and everything ugly.

But only she would go on destroying.

Felicity used to unintentionally direct her wrath at others, but she started to lose people she loved that way. If she got high, she would only hurt herself. So, she gave in to one-night stands with strangers and ended up hurting Jonathan instead because she didn't love him that way. She couldn't love him the way he loved her. "I have three condoms so that means you have three chances to get it right." None ever did. Afterward, the douche, soap and water, was always her birth control with breakfast. There was one week between the sex and a visit to a free clinic for a test and two weeks between the sex and a visit to a separate clinic for another set of tests and a pregnancy test as well. There was always a small, nagging disappointment when the pregnancy test would come up negative.

Felicity Woods, you are not mother material.

Her sisters argued that she would be if she slowed herself down. "But somehow," Ebony would grin, "I don't see that happening." "You always side with her. Both of you have always been in trouble," old and wise Mahogany would follow.

In a way, they were both correct. Ebony used to join Felicity in fights and troublemaking. She knew full well how careless Felicity could be since she'd often join her in an attempt to pick up the pieces. Ebony's experience as a troublemaker was amateur, and she was sobered too soon by an early pregnancy and an early marriage. Ebony and Mahogany's pregnancies scared Felicity out of motherhood.

Felicity made a mental note to call Ebony and tell her she was at it again.

As she stared in the mirror in the bathroom, she recalled one of her most recent escapades. The room was dark, and she couldn't make him out. Obviously, he was tall with fair brown skin. A look at his hair brought the night rushing back.

She was at a nightclub, and his tall figure approached her. "My name is Mario," and she ran her fingers through his hair.

"I love your hair," she said. She was drunk, and she knew it.

Then, he was in her ear, "Come outside and you can touch me some more," and she felt his breath on her neck. She knew what would happen and what she wanted, so she joined him.

Her clothes seemed far away, but she got up and tiptoed across the room. She got dressed quickly and quietly, making so little noise that she almost scared herself after she caught her shadowy reflection in the mirror. Her hair was long in those days, dripping down her back in curls that she never had under control. She remembered her intentions from the night before – get drunk and find a guy. *Check.* It was a good night. *Not too many personal items to search for in that case.* She straightened up herself after she retrieved her phone and small wallet.

Mario stirred in the bed. She ran out the door.

Outside, she did an inventory; she'd managed to pick up everything that she brought. She checked her phone and unsurprisingly found ten texts from an apologetic Jonathan. He'd never wait for her to apologize; he always took the blame and the guilt especially when she was wrong. He loved her too much. She sent a text back "yes" in response to his last exasperated text: "work on term paper?" All the love he gave her made some of her bitterness melt away, and she suddenly wasn't so sure she made the right decision the night before.

When she returned to her apartment, Jonathan was already waiting outside. The routine began: he offered a weak smile, open arms, and she would walk to him with a half-playful, half-regretful smirk; they'd finally embrace, she'd smell him and be happy he was there for security's sake; the two would go inside, and she'd cry a little and confess the night's activities. He would tell her he knew, and he would hold her until she fell asleep or stopped; she would get up and take her birth control, and he would object quietly.

Jonathan always wanted to start a family. He followed her to college to maintain their relationship and to prove that point. He didn't even want her to go to college; he, himself, wanted to take care of her. Felicity, however, didn't want to end up like her sister Ebony. They were seniors now, and while Felicity was unsure of her English degree, he was in line to be one hell of a surgeon. "Smart match, you and that guy," Mahogany would chide. "And the babies would be gorgeous; you can't forget that part," Ebony would laugh.

This time, though, he wasn't so quiet about the birth control.

"Don't take that pill, Li. You know I hate those things."

"I'm taking the pill, Jonathan." She threw it back quickly. He'd snatched one from her before. She noted that he was increasingly violent these days. "Besides, you know we can't just start a family. What kind of mother would I be? I can't even be faithful to you."

Felicity watched his face shift, and she knew she had hurt his feelings. There was no filter – she said what she meant. The last time that she had hurt his feelings, he pinned her to the bed and forced himself onto her, shaking her like a rag doll and yelling. She'd cried tears of panic during the whole two-minute affair. It was like getting a whipping as a child, and it was eerie with his face looming over her, a sheet of pure rage. When he stopped and looked at the panic and fear in her face, he sat up quickly and started shaking and didn't know what had happened. He cried, too, saying he was sorry and confused and that everything seemed to have gone black. It was his first display of violence against her. Yet again, out of some past-founded and compulsory need to protect him, she held him tightly, still crying and trying to understand. She felt that she would always be trying to understand.

"I wouldn't stick around to make it work with you if I didn't think you were going to try to make it work, too."

"Jonathan, stop it! It's not going to happen!"

Felicity had never raised her voice at him before, but she was extremely exasperated with the same argument, and she hastily concealed the fact that she scared herself.

"No," he said.

There was something dark in his face that she couldn't read. She wasn't afraid, though she should have been; Jonathan was six feet, three inches and a solid two hundred and fifty pounds. Next to him, she was very small.

"Just leave." Her voice betrayed her. There was danger brewing, and she could feel it in the way that he was looking at her. She wondered vaguely if he was even aware of her.

"I'm not going anywhere," Jonathan responded.

He moved a bit closer to her, clenching and unclenching his hands into fists. She put her hands up defensively, barely touching him but gauging how close they were.

"Please, just sit down."

Jonathan paused, his face shifting, and he appeared to try to discern what she was thinking and what was going on. He blinked his eyes solidly, becoming aware for the first time of what was happening. Reluctantly, he sat down. *Okay, he's calming down.* He glared at her and then buried his face in his hands. She saw the first tear hit the floor; it was the second time she'd ever seen him cry. *It's now or never. You could be stuck with him forever.* She composed herself and thought quickly of everything she needed to say and everything she'd been waiting to admit.

"Jon. We have to end this. I can't be with you anymore, not as hard as you love me and definitely not with your blacking out and forgetting."

He'd begun to sob, and the sound could have made the hardest of hearts break.

"I know," he managed.

His tears were pitiable, but she couldn't muster enough feeling to care. She walked over slowly, still unsure of his emotional state, until she finally stood in front of him and put her hands on his shoulders while he rested his head on her belly.

"I will still love you, Felicity. I will never stop loving you."

There was a strain of sadness, and the honesty nearly floored her. She knew that fifty years from now, Jonathan would come running if she called and that it would be torturous to continue their friendship. Still, she needed him and knew they would have to go through the motions. Unable to bear the thought and the responsibility inherent to her position, a single tear made its way down her face.

35

UNFINISHED PROJECTS

"I know, Johnny boy. I know."

Chapter 5

Six minutes passed, and Anthony was still at the table alone. He couldn't help but anxiously watch the restroom door. He didn't pin her to be the type to stand anyone up, and he hoped she would prove him wrong. *She's been in her thoughts the whole night, Ant. Let this go and just wait.* He pushed his glass back and forth between his hands. When he glanced up a second time, Felicity was standing next to the table.

"Wait," he said.

Felicity stopped, tilting her head to the left in confusion. Anthony looked at her and grinned. It was the first time that night he really saw what she was wearing. She'd changed her earrings, but everything about her had him baffled. He noticed quickly the details and let her sit down. He saw the smile on her face, and he knew she was trying to read his mind.

"The waitress still hasn't been by?"

"No." He said it too quickly. But she didn't seem to mind.

"Let's go. I'm not really hungry any more. Do you like ice cream?" She was talking fast, too, and she already had one hand on her purse.

"Yes," he smiled and stood, picking up his jacket and taking her arm. "Chocolate."

37

She turned up her head and smiled at him. Then, she tugged his arm, and they were out of the door.

It was the first full smile she'd given him, and it set his senses on fire. Her square, white teeth gleamed beneath her perfect pink gums and full brown lips. As they walked, her eyes were twinkling and gleaming on their own, not a streetlight around to make them sparkle, and he saw the mischief. *Gamine.* He wanted to kiss her. He wanted to pull her in tight. Would she object? They were outside, almost alone. He'd left a twenty dollar bill on the table without thinking even though they didn't have anything but water. No one would see them, but, then again, that really wasn't his concern.

"Are you going to kiss me?"

There it was, the permission he needed to taste those lips that beguiled him from the first time he saw her. It wasn't her legs; it was all of her that he wanted to lay siege to. He put his arms around her slowly and pulled her in. *She's so small.* Suddenly, there was an explosion and light show. He felt the fireworks of his mouth on hers, the teeth parting to make way for the tongue, and the hands around his neck. Sparks were running through him, and he felt his blood rise to his face. It felt as though it lasted forever. He hoped that it would. He didn't want to open his eyes unless she told him that he could. Her tongue and the gleam of her eyes had enslaved him.

38

UNFINISHED PROJECTS

Felicity stood on her toes and pressed her forehead against his. Even in her heels, he towered over her. "Did you feel that?" He felt so many things, and he couldn't place one idea, so he offered the simplest answer. "Yes." She had opened her eyes, and he could feel her looking at him. *Please don't let me be bright pink right now.*

"Come on," she breathed and smiled that timeless smile again.

She had his hand in hers, and she was pulling him, almost running. He followed her lead, and he knew that he would probably always be more than willing to for the rest of his life. *She's got power over you, and you've known each other for less than two weeks. You're a mess, Anthony.*

His mess had very little to do with anything. She had completely disarmed him. Any small amount of control he was used to having in his life was stripped away by that smile, that voice, and the way she said his name. Her shining eyes were like diamonds in the dark, wide and entrapping. He wanted to be engulfed in the small brown pools of clay, to build castles out of them, and to sculpt something beautiful and permanent for her to behold always. You wouldn't have known he was featured on the cover of *Fortune* a year ago as she dragged him through the busy street like a child.

They were laughing like children, and people were moving out of their way, smiling at them. *I could get used to this.*

"The place is right around the corner."

"What place?"

"Don't worry about it." She winked at him again. He almost swooned. *What on earth did I do to deserve this?*

It was a small Italian place, a hole in the wall that anyone could pass by, and it wasn't ice cream. It was gelato. *Even better.*

"Chocolate, right?"

Anthony nodded. Felicity started to speak, but distracted as he was by her hand holding his, it wasn't until she finished speaking that he realized she was ordering in Italian. He picked up a few cognates, "gelato" and "chocolate" among them. His foreign language proficiency was limited at best.

She speaks another language, too? You've got yourself a winner.

"Joe cay row one piece-o day pastel." Anthony's last girlfriend, Charlotte, was a spoiled girl from old Southern money. Her talents amounted to nothing more than artfully manipulating men. Her Spanish was offensive. She wanted to get engaged to the next rich man willing, but Anthony wasn't interested. She looked at him and saw a price tag, not a man. "But, daddy, don't you want your lovergirl forever?" It was the most insincere and nauseating display of affection he had ever borne witness to, let alone experienced, and the show was all for him. *Not in a million years.*

"How long have you spoken Italian?"
"Same amount of time I've been speaking Spanish, I guess. I'd say around ten years."
"Ten?"
"Yes. Ten. I've been speaking both since I was sixteen."
She grinned at him, and he felt his knees give way.

Chapter 6

"You're late," Jonathan growled, leaving the door open and barely casting a glance at his visitor.

"I assume she called you again." She closed the door slowly and locked it, dropping her purse and coat on the floor. She wouldn't be there long if she intended to score in time for the weekend.

He nodded, slowly and grimly. "She did."

Damn Felicity, still living in his head like a tumor.

Jasmine Jefferson's deep hatred of Felicity Woods was no secret in school. In fact, it was the highest form of entertainment. They fought and were sent home from school at least once a month only to fight more on the way out of the door. All the Woods sisters jumped Jasmine one night after a party when she said they would end up whores because their mother died. Ironically, Jasmine was the whore, and her mother was still living. The Woods girls didn't feel like pointing that out at that particular point in time though.

Furthermore, Jasmine was always plotting her way to Jonathan. Felicity was rarely honest with Jonathan, and she only loved him out of a need to protect him, but she would never lose him to a "two-bit heifer like Jasmine." Every time a fight erupted, Jonathan stood there, waiting for the first swing. They all knew it would come from Felicity.

UNFINISHED PROJECTS

Jasmine clawed and kicked, eventually landing some of the blows on Jonathan's back or neck, hurting him and further angering Felicity.

"You stupid little slut! You hit him!"

Jonathan tossed Felicity over his shoulder and carried her away from the fight to calm her down, and Jasmine stood there, defeated. Jasmine never wanted to hurt Jonathan. She was obsessed with him. Jonathan Michael Davis, the Adonis. She fantasized about him, thought about him while she was with other boys, and imagined he was inside her and touching her while underneath someone new. He was perfect in every way. "But no," her mother Lela would sneer, "he wouldn't want a whore like you when he could have a decent girl like Felicity. At least she keeps her legs closed."

It was the truth; Felicity and Jonathan lost their virginity together the night after senior prom. Incidentally, Jasmine went to the prom alone and ended up sleeping with Derek "Douche" Daniels afterward. He ran through more girls at school than anyone else. As he left, rushing to get back home and shoving his shirt carelessly into his pants, he said, "He'll never want you, really. You're just a waste of yellow as he is."

Was that what she was? A waste?

No. That's just Douche talking and a bad memory playing tricks. That's not true.

UNFINISHED PROJECTS

Still, as Jonathan plowed further and further into her tonight, biting her and pulling her hair, Jasmine couldn't help but think that maybe Derek Daniels was right.

Chapter 7

"It's getting kind of late. I need to get to bed so I can serve the Tyrant tomorrow."

They walked the block and made their way back to the Del Frisco's where Anthony's car was still parked.

"Let me take you home."

Anthony was aware that he looked a little childish, the spoon sticking out of his mouth, bobbing up and down as he spoke. It was crushed between his teeth since he finished his gelato. Felicity gave him her full smile again, and his eyes widened.

"It's okay," she whispered, "I'll call a cab or something."

He was offended that the idea even crossed her mind that he would allow her to rely on someone else to take her home. He saw the look in her eyes, the dashing back and forth, and her indecision about something she was keeping to herself. He made the decision for her.

"You will not take a cab while I'm right here, a more than able-bodied driver with gas in my car."

"It's the able body part that I'm worried about." She glanced warily at him.

He didn't think it was possible, but she looked flushed, and there was a sexual nervousness and tension she produced and transferred to him. *She*

45

just made a pass at you, Anthony. Subtle, but she's sizing you up again and you know it. Her eyes were roving over his frame. He promised that one day he'd allow her mouth to do the same – just not today. He couldn't do that today.

"Let me take you home, Felicity."

She sighed. *Was that relief?* He would have to further analyze her sighs to make sure.

"Okay."

Anthony held the door open for her and closed it behind her the way a gentleman should. As he made his way around the car, he muttered a short prayer for restraint before he got into the driver's seat. The ride to her apartment was a short one, but the awkward silence made it almost unbearable. He could feel her look at him, hear her draw in a breath as though she wanted to speak, but then she released it and stayed silent.

Finally, "I had a good time this evening." It didn't sound genuine. She was trying to play it cool and be smart, still reading him.

"I'm glad you did," he smiled. She smiled, too. "Would you be willing to get together again sometime?"

She started fidgeting uncontrollably now. "I would. Would you?"

"My offer was sincere, darling. I'd love to see you again." Anthony felt his temperature rising. He always tried to avoid that one word if he could, but he wanted to ease her mind. *That was a careless mistake, Anthony. She might not like you, and you go around using that word.*

Then, "I'd love to see you again, too, soon." He'd just parked outside of her apartment, and they were face to face.

Anthony put his hand up to her cheek and played with her ear, allowing his fingertips to mingle in her hair. Felicity smiled and then giggled flirtatiously blinking her eyes, slowly drinking in his facial features. He leaned in, pressing his head against hers and felt the cool of her forehead. Her hand was wrapped around his wrist, and she squeezed it as though she would lose her balance if she let him go. Slowly, quietly, he kissed her.

"I don't think I will ever get enough of that feeling," she whispered.

"I can't get enough of you." There were sparks still flying in his mind. Her reaction told him she felt the same.

The twinkle in her eyes told him that he was entering an entirely different realm.

"Come in with me? Please?" Now she was changed again, a different energy and a hint of loneliness in her voice.

He was fighting every male impulse he had, his groin taking on a mind of its own. *What would it be like? What would she taste like? I know I could make you happy, baby!*

47

"I can't. I can't do that. It's disrespectful." *Damn my southern manners.*

"Oh." She looked wounded. She slowly pulled away from him, but she still held on to his hand.

"Okay." She abruptly loosed him and opened the door.

"No, wait."

He threw his door open and ran around the car to hold open hers. She was almost out of the car by the time he got there.

"It's okay. I can get out of the car alone. I'm a big girl, you know." Another attitude shift – now she was almost angry. *She doesn't do well with rejection.*

"Don't be mad. Look, I didn't mean to offend you, Felicity. I just don't want to move too fast. I really like you, and I don't want to mess this up." He was blown away and flustered simultaneously. Maybe she was used to dealing with one kind of guy.

Felicity stood, her face blank, eyes burning a hole into nowhere with her nose in the air. She didn't look at him once. When she finally did, it was with a coolness she didn't have before.

"Have a good night and drive safely, Anthony." Then, she turned on her heels and walked away.

He wasn't going to let her win that easily. He allowed her to walk, putting distance between her and the car. When he opened his car door and was about to get in, he shouted, "By the way, your

African earrings are just as gorgeous as those pearls."

Felicity swung around, a wild look in her eyes. Anthony grinned like a fool and prepared himself in case she gave chase. Right before she turned around, he thought he saw a smile on her face. *No time to figure that out, Casanova. Go home.*

When he returned to his own place, he felt as if it was too quiet. Her giggle had been bouncing around in his mind the whole ride home replete with her perfect Italian accompanied by images of her smile. He called in a favor.

"White ones. Yes. Two dozen. Okay. Thanks."

The next morning, she would wake up to flowers in case he had really managed to offend her although he knew he didn't. He'd come to a conclusion about their relationship on her behalf – he would court her, and if she wanted to keep him around, she would have no choice but to respect his wishes not to intrude on her after their dates.

Anthony had courted Charlotte, as well, but he made the mistake of telling her so after the second date. "Oh, you're going to court me? Well, we are going to make this a long engagement because I'm not cheap, daddy."

Anthony spent a small fortune on Charlotte, waiting on her hand and foot to discover that she was a hopeless and stubborn prude of below

49

average intelligence. She didn't even want to kiss him in public, let alone hold his hand. She often resorted to mindless prattle at the dinner table, and she would publicly deny him on days she decided his outfit was beneath her standard.

"You didn't even try, Anthony," her southern drawl making every word heavier and burdensome. "Don't you want to try a little bit harder for me?"

No. No, I really don't. But he would never say aloud something like that to her. He wasn't even sure what attracted them to each other in the first place. Even his mother thought she was a snob, and she would say as much to him whenever he visited her in Mississippi.

"She's haughty and arrogant and not at all worth your effort, honey." Anthony loved the way his mother put him on a pedestal, always a bit more proud of him than he felt he deserved. She always liked him more than she liked her older sons but, as a mother, expressing preference for one child over the next is dangerous. They felt it but never said anything; his brothers were his father's sons, only.

Quit fidgeting, Anthony. If you want to call the girl, just do it. He was in the apartment fifteen minutes and kept staring at the phone. He wanted to call her, talk, and maybe hear her giggle. Text messages would no longer suffice after their first date.

UNFINISHED PROJECTS

"Hello, this is the voicemail of Felicity Woods, head assistant to James Jeffries...." *Damn.* He was more fearful than before he'd offended her. He called a second time and got the busy tone; she was on the other line. *The flowers may be my only redeeming point.*

It was the curves and the smile and the eyes and the hair and the arms and everything about Felicity Woods that had his head spinning. He didn't want to be inside with his own thoughts tonight. He had to talk to someone.

Chapter 8

"You're gonna have to leave now. I hate to kick you out and all, but you're really going to have to go." Jones had her shirt in his hand and slowly extended it to her.

"Are you really kicking me out? Wow. You really don't give a damn about anyone but yourself." She hastily snatched the shirt from him, a glint of humor in her expression.

Jones rolled his eyes and walked away. The speech being delivered now sounded dreadfully like the speech he got yesterday. All of the women he entertained said the same things. They'd come in and be blown away by the size of his apartment, ask why he had so much space to himself, make love in every corner of the apartment, and he'd tell them, when they ended up in his bedroom, "That's why." The next morning, if he liked her enough to keep her overnight, she'd wake up in the bed alone and find him at his desk where he'd briskly ask her if she needed a ride home, and if she didn't, he sent her on her way.

Melody was one such young lady he would let stay over more than once. He enjoyed and preferred her company. He realized too late that this was a mistake. She developed a sense of entitlement after her first visit. Now, she was nagging him about their quickest encounter yet – thirty minutes of unbridled fun.

"Yeah, well, I don't have time for you to be here right now," he frowned, his patience wearing thin, "I have someone else coming over." Jones then turned away from Melody because he couldn't lie to her face.

"So, you call me over for sex, and then you kick me out for some other chick. You're a sick bastard, Jones. Don't ever call me again." Just like that, half-dressed and furious, Melody slammed the door and left.

"Good riddance." He didn't really have a girl coming over, but he was tired of Melody and her whining. She'd be back next week, half naked under a trench coat, to apologize. Truthfully, as long as Melody was alive, Jones would never go wanting. It was only when he wanted what he didn't get enough of as a child that he called women like Melody and put up with their noise. And the past two loveless weeks were enough to drive him insane.

That girl knew I was staring at her, he started hitting his wall, *and she was busy staring at Ant.*

It was years of jealousy and loneliness talking, Anthony always taking the pretty girls in college and claiming he only thought of them as friends. "Does she know that you're 'just' friends?" Jones would say and Anthony would shrug. "I don't know.

I should probably tell her." Anthony would smile sheepishly, genuinely uncertain. A few of the girls would then tiptoe back to Jones, and he would gladly take the unsuspecting seconds until the next pretty girl wanted Anthony's attention.

Now, some secretary ignored him in front of a room full of his higher colleagues, and he didn't get the opportunity to hit on her because Anthony wanted to leave the meeting early. *You let him leave his card, too. You let him get to her first.* Jones didn't even know her name, but he knew he had dibs. *Besides*, he reasoned, *she's black. Why would she talk to a guy like Ant, anyway? She'll make the right decision soon. She'll change her mind. She'd better.*

The ringing phone yanked him back to the present, his stomach churning, and a headache forming. He dismissed it as hunger and answered the phone, opening the refrigerator in search of a post-sex snack. "Hello."

"Jones."

"Ay, Ant. What's up man?" *The last person I want to talk to right now.*

"You remember that girl from Jeffries' place?"

"Yeah, what's up?" *The last thing I want to talk about right now.*

"I just dropped her off. We went out for dinner. Well, we never really got the dinner. More like a trip out for ice cream. Actually, it was gelato. She speaks Italian. Do you know anyone who speaks Italian?"

UNFINISHED PROJECTS

Anthony's enthusiasm was palpable, even over the phone, and Jones felt himself getting hot. If they had gone on a date, she wouldn't have changed her mind.

"So, you had that woman all to yourself tonight, and you didn't think to call me beforehand? You know you mismanage these opportunities. You with her now?"

"No, I wanted to see if you wanted to get together for a drink or something."

Jones would never understand his friend, how he could make all the classic mistakes and not take the opportunity with a girl like that the first night. "Why didn't you jump on that?"

There was silence on the other line. Jones knew Anthony was trying not to say something rude like, "Not everyone is like you, Jones," or, "You're the only one who finds that appropriate." Anthony was always trying to tell him how to behave when it came to women, and it was getting annoying. One of the many things he disliked about Anthony was his ownership of the largest part of their company; it made him feel as though he had to act according to another man's whims.

"I will talk to you later, Jones. Call up one of your girls and have a good night." He wasn't prepared for such a measured response.

Jones couldn't hide his shock. "You aren't going to just hang up on me, white boy!" It was too late.

UNFINISHED PROJECTS

Jones shouted over the click, and his response was the empty dial tone.

    Fuck.

Chapter 9

"I promise you that this time is so different, Ebbs. He's sweet, caring, pays attention to detail, and he didn't even want to sleep with me tonight!"

"He wanted to sleep with you. He just had the good sense to show restraint."

"Ebbs, what's wrong with you? You sound tired."

"I have five children, Li. How the hell am I supposed to sound?"

"I mean you sound angry. What's up with you?"

There was a pause. A door closed somewhere in the house, and there was a series of footsteps. "I've got to go. He's home."

"Ebbs?" The phone clicked before Felicity could utter another word.

"Who were you on the phone with just now?" He wasn't very close to her; the shadows cast, obscuring his face.

"No one, honey. Just Felicity. I told her earlier that I would have to get off the phone when you got home so I could warm up your dinner."

He sniffed, and through the shadows, she saw his eyes, wide and angry. He always seemed to be angry these days. The children were all in bed, but the house was loud and noisy with static radiating off of him. His anger, heat, and abusive nature joined his noise in an echo through the house; with it were the words, the things that she should have said to the police but didn't, and her children's cries of panic.

Ebony was never a big girl, taking after her mother in frailty and thinness. She was easy to carry, even when she was first pregnant and her ankles declined to swell. Biggs would hold her in his arms and carry her upstairs to bed or pick her up from the bathroom floor when morning sickness got the better of her.

"Thank you, Big." She'd smile, weak from the dry heaves and shivering slightly.

"It's what I'm here for, baby," and he'd kiss her forehead, rubbing his nose against her.

After their third child was born, Biggs stopped being as sweet about many things, and she had to carry herself back to their bedroom.

Biggs was a semester from graduating college when they met. He studied business and marketing and acquired a good job working for a major oil company. Ebony was fortunate to have him since she was just graduating from high school when she got pregnant, and everyone said that she kept the first baby to trap him. She was only seventeen when she broke the news to her family. Biggs would beat down any man or boy who said a cross word and glare at any girl who had the nerve to stare. He loved Ebony. His mother argued with him and tried to make him reconsider. Secretly, Ebony wondered if reconsidering would then mean that he wouldn't be beating her down every night fourteen years later.

"I said what did Felicity want?"

Suddenly, Biggs was very close. Ebony had allowed herself to think of happier times when she should have been paying attention to his closing proximity. His eyes were red in the corners, and his shoulders seemed to be larger than usual.

"She just wanted to talk about some guy she is dating."

"Sure." Biggs moved in closer. If she ran, he'd chase her, and it would be worse. She allowed herself to be cornered, pinned between him and the kitchen wall, stuck in her seat at the table.

"Where are the kids?"

"Upstairs, sleeping."

"Get up and go to bed. You look tired."

Ebony did as she was told, standing very slowly and keeping eye contact with him. She didn't blink, which left her face blank with fear, staring into his angry hazel eyes.

"Go to bed, Ebony."

Her surprise wasn't easily hidden. She let her shoulders drop, and she exhaled quietly. She still hadn't blinked.

"Okay."

But she was stuck between him and the chair, and he wouldn't move aside so that she could push in the chair.

Ebony's thoughts jolted back to the first time that he hit her. Biggs had pulled her head back and slammed it into the table; then, he had hit her across the opposite side of the head with the back of his hand while she was screaming in agony after the first blow.

Now, she tried to shift her legs again, and he had his eyes glued on her, his face a mask of sheer rage.

"Excuse me, sweetheart," she whispered.

"What?" He was too quiet.

"Excuse me."

"Are you stupid or something? I told you to go to bed."

"I can't; you're too close. I'm stuck."

"Don't talk back to me!"

Twice, Ebony felt the sting from the back of his hand, one on each side. Biggs pulled her hair back, forced her back into the chair, and wrenched her head back so she would look up at him. He had a sickening grin on his face.

Through watery vision, out of the corner of her eye, Ebony caught a glimpse of the stairs, her oldest daughter standing with the youngest on her hip, the three boys peeking through the banister, all in pajamas with tears streaming down their beige and copper faces.

UNFINISHED PROJECTS

Her name was Ebony Woods, mother of five with two black eyes.

Chapter 10

"We should go cow tipping."

"I'm sorry, what?"

"You know, when it's dark and you go push the cow over, and it lays there on the ground until it wakes up?"

"Do cows sleep on their feet?"

"I'm pretty sure they do. They were always asleep when I was a kid."

"You had a past life as a baby goat?"

There was the smirk, the playful tug at her chin, and finally, "No, smart ass."

Felicity was irrevocably in love with Anthony Bruce James, the man with three first names from Mississippi and a mind like Einstein. Why he was shy with her when they first saw one another at her job, she'd never know. Now, he seemed to be the only one who was open about everything – about how he wanted her and when, about how much he loved her smile and the way that she thought he was a funny white boy, about how she was his first thought every morning.

After their first date, he sent her white roses, and every date since their first, she woke up to a new bouquet. She retrieved a pot of dirt one day, and now she had lilies growing in her kitchen.

UNFINISHED PROJECTS

They'd finally made love after their seventh date. Was it a date? It seemed as if he was always stopping by at her office, cooking for her, albeit with difficulty, driving her home, and taking her to the movies. One day he showed up and told the Tyrant that she needed a break and that his own secretary would stand in on her behalf. At the time, Jeffries nearly turned purple but couldn't object; in retrospect, it was the funniest moment in her five-year employment at J. Parts.

When they stepped outside, she'd asked him, "Are you even allowed to do that?" Anthony shrugged it off. "I own half of his company, too," he had responded.

There was another admirable trait – *as if his list isn't brimming*; he never made her feel small or under obligation because of money. She never asked or thought twice about the places they went to eat. He let her pay for half once because she threatened to put him in a choke hold. It was his birthday, after all. The day after their fourth date, he brought her a set of pearls – "to match those earrings of yours." He stood behind her as she placed them in her ears, and he was studying her face in the mirror; it was brewing with a mixture of thankfulness and worry. She wanted to know what she'd done to deserve them. He smiled at her – *God, those eyes* – and said, "You don't have to do anything for me but smile."

63

UNFINISHED PROJECTS

The old Felicity would have scoffed, especially if it were Jonathan doing the talking. She would have dismissed him and called him a liar because, if it were anyone else, he would have been lying. Anthony wasn't just anybody.

"This is our eighth date."
"Cow tipping is part of our eighth date?"
ZZ Top was playing from the small radio he brought to their little picnic, and the rugged voice of the lead carried on about his head being in Mississippi. *Funny, he didn't say anything about where his heart might be.*
"Absolutely," he laughed. She loved that laugh so much.
"Well, if it ends anything like our seventh date, I'm fine. Cow tipping it is." Anthony looked down at her, his eyes shining. "This song is growing on me," Felicity added, hurriedly.
It was quiet and peaceful at the park where they were spread out on a blanket that he brought from his apartment. She was holding his hand, gazing up at him, eyes wide.
"I wish every night ended like our seventh date," and he kissed her forehead.
"Come stay with me, then." She'd brought up an old argument.
"I won't. You know I won't. I'm the man; you need to stay with me if we're talking about moving

in together, and I don't want that for us yet. Slow and steady, pretty lady." Felicity loved it when he sounded Southern.

"So, will you let me move in, then?" She wouldn't drop it.

Anthony tilted his head back, his eyes were wide with shock, and he drew a quick breath. It was on their sixth date when she told him that she'd gladly take him home to her father. The shock showed in his face, even as he tried to laugh it off and disregard the surprise. It was just like that now.

"You really want that?"

"Yes, I do. I want to stay with you."

"Do you love me?"

It was her turn to be shocked. Couldn't he tell? Had all the years of sleeping around done that much to her emotions, or was it something deeper? Was she hiding that much from him? She couldn't properly display love if even he didn't know that she loved him. Why would he ask if he knew? Was this just a test? *Oh no.*

"Say what you're thinking, Felicity."

"I thought you already knew."

"Knew what?"

"That I love you." Felicity was scared, and she felt tears collecting in her eyes.

"Of course I knew. I can feel it. But hearing you say it means more to me than it does in your mind.

It means so much to hear it because it shows that you trust me with your thoughts."

Anthony's eyes were getting watery, his big sea green eyes. It was a feature of his that Felicity loved; she imagined his tears collecting in some far off abyss, her doing a backstroke in that sea green. She didn't want him to cry. She kissed him.

"Baby, I will gladly say it a thousand times. I promise I will." He nodded, resting his forehead against hers. She loved being in this place, in this quiet place alone with him. He meant everything to her.

"I love you so much, Felicity. I have since day one."

"I know, Ant. I know."

For the first time ever, she wanted the love to last.

Chapter 11

She watched them from the driver's seat; her shades perched high on her nose, lenses so dark it felt like the midnight hour. She'd taken care to park on the other side of the street, a place where she wouldn't be seen but she could observe freely. They seemed so happy, the man with a baby in one arm, the woman softly cooing to another, smiling and unaware. Between them was nothing but locked fingers and a myriad of secrets. The couple loved one another, and it was obvious in their smiles.

Why me, Father? Why did I have to be the one?

It seemed like forever since he'd last been to her door, but seven years wasn't really that long. He'd come with a check and an apology, a handshake but no time for a hug. The baby wasn't a baby anymore; she was eight years old, large as a house and looking every bit like her father. The child wasn't supposed to be looking or listening, but she sat at the top step and peered down to the doorway.

He loomed in the doorway. "I can't keep seeing you like this. I can't see you anymore. Just stay away. This money is for the kid; I will send enough to last until she's eighteen. I don't want to hear from you again."

His words were cold and finite. She didn't protest because she was already defeated. She took the heavy manila envelope, stuffed with thousands of dollars, a first installment that she wouldn't have the heart to put in an account for a month. Her heart felt as if it was in her throat, but she couldn't open her mouth to object. She felt his eyes blazing into her and imagined for a moment that he was as sad as she was. With her eyes cast to the floor, she did nothing more than nod.

"My lawyer will drop off more money next month."

He turned around and walked out the door. Slowly, an inhuman sound rose from deep within her. She'd never heard a sound like it before. At twenty-nine, she was moaning. There was a dry heave that put a pause in the noise that filled the small foyer and most of the house, and she heard the stair creak under the weight of her daughter.

"Momma, are you okay?"

Mahogany couldn't even look up at her baby girl, the one to whom she'd devoted so much time and life and the one she'd kept because he begged her to. It was frightening that she looked so much like her father with those big brown eyes with gray rings around the edges, that wide, flat nose, ears that she would have to grow into, and a thin upper lip. How could she face Maxine – so named because his name is Max – with what just happened?

"Momma is gonna be okay," she said more to herself than Maxine, "Momma is going to fix us up nice for church tomorrow."

"Church?"

"Yes, honey, church. You've avoided going long enough."

"I thought you said church was full of phonies and that you only went to ease your troubled soul."

She faced her daughter for the first time, clutching the envelope of money close to her chest. A weak smile made its way to her face. Leave it to your own child to keep you honest. Unfortunately, honesty is also a swift call to anger between mother and child.

"You're absolutely correct, honey. Momma said exactly that. But now Momma says different, and you like doing what Momma says because you get whipped when you don't. Isn't that right?"

Maxine retreated in fear. She hated having to threaten her like that, especially when the poor child had only been whipped once. Maxine was a good girl, more than any mother could ask for in the way of obedience. She always minded her manners and tried to eat politely at the table. She smiled and said hello to all adults, and she rarely questioned anyone's authority. Her one and only weakness was eavesdropping. The one time that Maxine got caught eavesdropping was the one time that she was whipped; she'd listened in on a phone conversation and later asked what "fucking" meant.

"Didn't-I-tell-you-not-to-listen-in-on-my-phone-calls?" every word in staccato, delivered with another blow, a strike with her hand, a belt or anything that she could reach at the moment. The ordeal lasted about thirty minutes longer than it should have.

When Max arrived later and discovered what happened, he was furious with both of them. "What sense does it make for you to beat her when you and I do what she asked about on a regular basis?"

The words stung in a deep place she couldn't name, and she suddenly felt like a hypocrite. She thought that they made love, but she came to realize that there was a difference between the way she was feeling and the way that he thought of her. *A married man is never going to love you the way he loves his wife.* She would hear her mother's voice in her head. *Don't ever chase after a married man.*

All of that happened seven years ago and what a difference the time had made. Maxine was wearing a real bra; she'd thinned considerably and let her hair grow relatively long. It felt unfair, her baby girl turning into a young lady. Maxine would be fifteen soon. She loved sports and art, and she excelled in both; funds from a mystery 'donor' made sure that she had the best sporting goods and the best art teachers.

Here she was, in the middle of the afternoon, sitting in a car and in a way, eavesdropping. The fact that Maxine would be waiting to get picked up for her piano lessons seemed distant, but she had to see him. For some odd reason, she had to see his wife, as well.

Did he ever tell her about you? Do they laugh at you? Does he still have other women he sees?

Of course, a man like Maxwell Powell never went wanting for long. It was his power that made her want him more. She was the new girl who wanted to be rescued from the world of work after years of caring for her younger siblings, and he was the perfect benefactor. It was the classic affair between employee and employer, one that other members of the office saw Mr. Powell take advantage of time and time again. They all knew that she would eventually be fired and that, sooner or later, another innocent woman would fall into the trap, but none ever spoke up. It didn't seem to be worth the effort.

"We're going to go to church every Sunday, and Momma is going to join the choir. Maybe the pastor will let you play the piano during service. Won't it be fun to be in the Lord's house?"

The idea was sounding better and better the more she said it as the conversation carried over to dinner. There was a time when she went to church every Sunday because her mother would have expected it. Times changed when she got older. She wasn't clutching the money anymore, but it was still right next to her dinner plate.

"How will you join the choir if rehearsal is at night and you work all day?" Maxine asked.

It was a good point. After she was fired for inappropriate behavior – *he was just embarrassed that everyone knew* – she reasoned she'd worked several jobs to keep her small condominium and put gas in her car. Everything else went to feeding her ever-growing child. That wouldn't be much trouble anymore.

"Momma isn't too worried about work anymore," and she inadvertently glanced at the envelope. Maxine's eyes also wandered over to the envelope. She wasn't naive enough to believe for a second that Maxine hadn't listened to every word of the conversation that preceded the one they were having now, but she knew to play along.

"What's that, Momma?"

"What's what?"

"The big envelope next to your plate."

The manila envelope called to both of them at once. It was huge and glowing and completely out of place; they both stared at it for a moment.

"This, my lovely, is your and Momma's meal ticket."

"We are already eating, Momma."

My poor baby is so innocent, she mused, smiling evenly at her child, *but she is going to have to learn*.

"Maxine, Momma is going to make you a promise, okay?" She leaned in conspiratorially, ready to impart some great secret.

The young girl's head bobbed slowly, ready to absorb all the information her mother volunteered.

"Every time we get one of these envelopes here," she said, lifting the object that was weighing heavily on both their minds, "she is going to put half of what's inside away for you, and the other half is going to be for anything else we want to do. How does that sound?"

"You mean like a vacation, Momma?" She was practically bouncing in her seat. "Can we go see Mickey Mouse?"

"We can see him and Minnie, too."

Her child was literally beaming at her after the good news.

In her pocket, she felt a small vibration. *Okay, baby, Momma is coming to get you now.*

The school was about a mile away, and she drove at a moderate speed, careful of the elderly on the road and the young. One thing she hated about driving was that she had to drive for everyone, taking into consideration those on all sides. When she drove Maxine to her first soccer game, another mother from the opposing team nearly tore off the passenger side of her car. It was the first time that she was grateful her eight year old was mindlessly kicking back her seat. *You have to drive for everybody when it's not just about you anymore.*

It was silent in the car but unbearably noisy in her mind. She turned on the radio and was pleasantly surprised when one of her old CDs began playing instead. There was something about Tchaikovsky's uproarious "1812" that set her mind at ease; it reminded her that there was a possibility for worse things to turn out beautifully. Her father made it a point to listen to classical music, and she did the same with Maxine who would try to change the station. "What would your grandfather say if you shut it off at his house?" and Maxine would quickly leave the stereo alone.

I should call Daddy when Maxine gets in the car.

Outside the school, Maxine stood, bags in tow: one for soccer, one for art, and one with school supplies. There were a few young boys standing nearby, staring at her until the car pulled up, and they all busied themselves with imaginary objects on the sidewalk. *That's right, boys. Keep your eyes off my daughter.* Maxine pulled at the back door as best she could, her hands slipping momentarily. With the door ajar, she loaded down the back seat with bags.

UNFINISHED PROJECTS

When they first bought the car, she didn't think that it would be necessary. As Maxine got older and taller and her extracurricular activities consumed both of their schedules, they were both increasingly grateful for the four-door, the all-wheel drive, and the massive trunk space.

"Hey, Momma." Maxine planted a kiss on her mother's cheek.

"Hey, baby. How was school today?"

As always, the conversation between them flowed easily. As they drove home, Maxine shared with her mother how she got another few A's on assignments and continued to top every classmate. When asked by Maxine, Mahogany told her daughter that she had an easy day working from home, transcribing documents for a small law firm at an hourly rate of seventeen dollars. Working from eight in the morning until seven at night three days a week and from eight until three the other two days allowed her more than enough time to meet every one of Maxine's needs.

"Maxi, come on down for church, honey!"

It was an early service, but she wanted to go. There was something tugging at her stomach and her heart, a mixture of guilt, need, and obligation that said church would be just the thing to set her mind at ease. She'd gone for five Sundays in a row and knew that this time would be different. God would make her clean, she'd be forgiven, and the merciless eyes of the church wouldn't tear at her soul. If that didn't happen, she would have to fake it.

"Ugh, Momma!" Without looking up the stairs, she knew Maxine was griping about the frills on her dress. "I hate these things! I want to tear them off."

"You look like a little angel with them on. Besides, that dress cost me too much to be tailored to fit you, dear. I'm not going to shred it because you're being a little self- conscious."

"You didn't pay for the whole thing."

"Don't get smacked, Maxine. Not on a Sunday."

Physical threats were the resort for exasperated parents and proved to be enough to temporarily silence Maxine, as her footsteps toward the door provided a hint that she would grin and bear the dress. In truth, she did look out of place, wrapped up in all of those frills and wide as a house.

When they returned home from church, giggling because of the 'religious experience' one of the women had during service, she went up to her room, making sure that Maxine was closed in hers. Under the bed was a box that she hadn't opened in a long time. For a while, she was afraid of what its contents would mean a year after their owner no longer cared to share his life with them.

"Momma, you're gonna drive past Madame Pettit's house! Slow down."

76

UNFINISHED PROJECTS

She swerved slightly and pulled into the elderly woman's driveway. Memory of the old shoebox sent her mind into a spiral.

There were only about five things in the box worth mentioning. The largest item was a thin shirt with his initials on the cuff. She was particularly fond of the smell. In her room, there was a small metal bin. She poured a bottle of perfume, another gift in the box, into the bottom of it and found a lighter in her drawer. Soon, the bottom of the bin was in flames.

After rising to open the window and to put the bin on the nude windowsill, she continued to offer burnt sacrifice of the past nine years of her life. The perfume and shirt were the first to go. Following closely behind were the broken pieces to a vase that he bought while he was on vacation in Japan with his wife. She figured it wouldn't burn, but she didn't want it anymore; it was a reminder of how broken she was and the fact that she was once carrying something beautiful on his behalf. She tossed it piece by piece into the bin. To her surprise, it did burn, melting down easily with the rest.

Without realizing it, she had started to cry with each piece. The past smelled like Chanel No. 5. A few miscellaneous items – knickknacks and small things he'd left behind – were slowly added to the pyre. She lifted a handkerchief and started to wipe

77

her face but thought better of it. It would have sent her to a place she was actively avoiding. It was unceremoniously tossed into the bin, the flames growing larger, the metal getting hot, and she wiped her face with the back of her hand.

The last item she pulled from the shoebox was a note that was older than Maxine. It was one of those cutesy offerings, something that used to appeal to her young mind even though it was typewritten.

"I can't take my eyes off of you."

"We should go to dinner sometime," he'd say.

"You are too sweet to be working for a mean man like me."

"I'd love to take you to dinner," he'd say it again as if she hadn't heard the first time or after she teasingly rejected him.

"I will be leaving my wife soon."

"I'm falling for you."

After re-reading the note and laughing bitterly at how easily she was deceived, she shed her last tear and dropped it into the fire. As the cinders flared and the final sacrifice let out a small hiss, into the flames went part of her heart; the words on the disintegrating paper read "MEMO: Mahogany."

Chapter 12

I never liked the old man, he thought angrily, taking his fifth shot. *I'd smile in his face all day if it meant he'd let me have her and stayed out of the way.*

There were only a few people in Smokey's bar, which was really just a hole in the wall somewhere in New Orleans, so Jonathan didn't feel a need to hide his alcoholism. The few patrons were standing on opposite ends of the small room. It was one of those easily disguised places that looked much smaller than it was from the outside but could be full to capacity with nosey people and good liquor on the right night.

Unencumbered, he ended up downing ten shots of whiskey and four beers. His head stopped spinning momentarily when he landed his eyes on a young woman at the end of the bar. She must have been watching him because the moment she saw him looking, she smiled.

The night is young, and I'll have merriment yet, he thought, bitterly.

She slid gracefully off the stool and walked over to him. From afar, he saw her strongest features; she had fair skin and blonde and brown hair, and he already wanted to sink his teeth into her legs.

Jonathan had become progressively violent with women over the years, adapting to the more harmful concepts associated with sexual activities like BDSM until he was simply brutal. His career expanded quickly after his residency, but so did his sex drive. Anything was possible in his room – handcuffs, chains, beatings – but he always ended up feeling lonely post-coital bliss.

She let her jacket hang open, and he saw all the curves, the lines of her body teasing him and a few other men, including Smokey.

"How have you been?"

Do I know her?

"I figured you wouldn't remember me. You always had your eyes on one girl in school."

Jonathan rolled his eyes and went back to sipping his beer. His head was clearing, and the more he looked at her, the more the memories rushed back. He mostly remembered a lot of fighting and a lot of taunting before when he knew her, but what rang truest to his dulled senses was the stories of her being under boy after boy. She was like an old dishrag that no one had the heart to discard. Every guy from school still talked about her, about how she thought there was some imaginary totem pole to climb to get to him. It was a flattering idea when he was younger, cute to an extent. However, he was never into her, and he didn't intend to start now. If she wanted to make him an offer, he wouldn't refuse, but he certainly wasn't going to reach out to her with open arms.

Besides, he was currently too drunk and angry to care.

"You know, Jasmine, as entertaining as it is to reminisce with you and all, I'm really not in the mood. You weren't on my mind then, and I don't really think you want to be on my mind now, no matter how much you profess to care and think about me the way you did back at school."

He heard her breathe in sharply, but he wouldn't look at her to see whether or not it was out of shock. He took another gulp of beer. Much of what he said was more cautionary, to make sure that he was still able to say no to a woman; he doubted his ability to protect women from his temper and sexual appetite. It surprised him how many women didn't care.

"That's too bad, Jonathan." She smiled or at least he thought she did. On closer inspection, she looked like a wounded puppy to him, but she wouldn't move. There was something strange about her behavior.

Will she really stand here and stare at me even though I just gave her that huge kiss off?

"You could slap me right now, and I wouldn't leave this bar unless I was leaving with you."

How she knew what he was thinking didn't matter. What did matter was the increasing tightness in his pants. He had commitments in the morning at the hospital, but he would make an exception; a patient willing to go under the knife was standing right beside him.

"I hope you remember, baby," he said, his voice suddenly deceptively sweet, "you get what you ask for."

Chapter 13

It's her curves and her smile and her eyes and her hair and her arms and her... everything that are making me absolutely crazy. The room isn't spinning – it's me. I'm reeling and lovesick and completely intoxicated. It's been five months, two weeks, and three days, and I've been high off of this woman the whole time. I've got an angel on my side. I hope she never leaves me.

The apartment was quiet as the two of them lay in bed. Felicity was sleeping beside him on her established side of the bed. She'd let her hair grow, and Anthony was happy she did; it was absolutely beautiful. She was absolutely beautiful. He was aware that he was watching her sleep, her chest barely moving; she was breathing deeply, controlled, and relaxed. She was always calm around him. They'd been out more times than he could count, but he didn't need to because she loved him.

She said she loves me!

He wanted to do a heel click. He'd never been this happy before.

There was something wonderful about having Felicity Woods all to himself, someone he could hold and who wouldn't object or pull away, who would hold his hand and cook for him. The idea of mutual love was something he never thought he'd experience.

A myriad of events from their time together sped through his mind – their first date, their first kiss, and the first time they made love in his bed – and now he had one more offer to make. He was sure that he wanted to be with her forever, and there was no time like the present to tell her. *No,* he thought to himself, *no time for doubt. This time next year, she will be Felicity James.*

The thought was thrilling. He was grinning to himself and had to stifle a laugh when she stirred slightly. He rose from the bed, careful not to disturb any of the sheets covering her sleeping form. As he stood up, staring down at her, she appeared even more beautiful than before.

Felicity James.

He smiled. Breakfast in bed would do. Quickly, he pulled on the jeans he'd left on the floor the night before and made his way to the open room that served as a kitchen, living room, and dining room. He started making plans in his head as he hastily pulled the refrigerator door open and removed all of the ingredients for an omelet, bacon, and some biscuits. The cabinet above the refrigerator had the grits.

I'm cooking for a girl. No, I'm cooking for my woman.

UNFINISHED PROJECTS

Anthony cracked open the eggs, chopped the peppers and onions, and then placed a skillet on the stove. *My woman is going to have whatever house she wants and wherever she wants it with a real living room, a real dining room, and a huge kitchen.*

The oven was warming; the eggs were cooking, the bacon was sizzling, and the biscuits were baking quickly.

Maybe she will want to move to California. She's always talking about California.

He pulled down a plate, stuffed the sautéed vegetables into the omelet with some cheese, and began to assemble the promising breakfast.

What about our honeymoon? I'm thinking everywhere in the Mediterranean. She's never left the country, which simply won't do.

The plate was piled high with food, and he was beaming at a job well done. All he needed now was some orange juice.

I want my woman to be seen by the world.

He lifted the plate and the orange juice. *Service with a smile.*

There were no limits to what he would do for this woman whom he loved. An unwelcome thought made its way into his mind from two nights before.

"You can't have what belongs to a man like me, Ant. What makes you think you deserve such a fine specimen?"

UNFINISHED PROJECTS

The venom in Jones' voice made his toes curl. Anthony knew his friend was possessive and that he'd made several passes at Felicity that night at the bar alone. She'd made her way to the ladies' room to "avoid the asshole," and Anthony only hoped that the comment was directed more toward Jones than to him. She told him time and time again that she didn't feel comfortable around Jones. Honestly, Anthony didn't feel comfortable leaving them together either.

Jones had a history with women, chewing them and spitting them back out like bad candy. He remembered their college days when Jones would ask for permission to "try" any and every girl he might have dated. A chill ran up his spine.

I would knock his teeth in if he even thought about that with Felicity.

It was supposed to be a pleasurable night, but the icy glare that Felicity gave him when she saw Jones in the bar would reverse global warming.

She pulled him in close by his lapels as though she intended to kiss him. "I thought you said that fucker wouldn't be here. What the hell is he doing here, Anthony?"

Even with Felicity's anger, it was hard to hide that he was turned on. He stifled a grin; she was wearing a murderous look. He put his hands in her hair, kissed her hard in the mouth, and pulled her head back abruptly.

86

"If he so much as looks at you sideways, we'll leave."

Two hours, eight rows of insults, and several drinks later, they were all still there. Anthony was standing between the two of them and caught all of the action first hand. Jones kept suggesting that Felicity wore the pants in the relationship, and Felicity offered that she at least had a relationship. Jones reminded her to watch her mouth, and Felicity said that was Anthony's job. Momentarily speechless, Jones replied that he was glad that a field hand like Felicity would at least have cute babies with a man like Anthony, and ever quick to quip, Felicity said that she'd rather have a real man than a sleazy Uncle Tom like his partner.

"Cut it the fuck out," Anthony commanded. Jones stopped out of shock, but Felicity wrapped her arms firmly around Anthony, leaning her head against him and closing her eyes.

"I told you I wanted to go," she whispered. She was one shot away from being drunk, and the more Anthony considered, the more he'd rather be in bed with her.

"Yeah, Anthony, run along with your mammy."

At this comment, Felicity yanked open her eyes, released Anthony, pushed him away with more force than either of them knew she had, and smacked Jones hard across the face. Before he could register that he'd been assaulted, she had him by the collar and slammed his head into the counter. Anthony got back to his feet. He couldn't believe what he was watching, what everyone in the bar was watching. Felicity looked as though she was going to strike again but sobered when she saw Anthony staring at her from the corner of her eye. She softened immediately – *Do I take her breath away, too? Get a grip, Anthony. She just beat the shit out of Jones* – and she lifted Jones off the bar where he was whimpering.

"Call me a mammy again," she said, "and I will beat you like your mammy should have."

Jones wanted to object. Anthony suspected that his jaw was broken.

Spectators, particularly black female spectators, broke into applause. Anthony thought he heard one of them say, "You go girl!" and he couldn't help but smile.

Outside the bar, he realized the gravity of what happened, but he didn't care. He wanted to keep it light. Felicity offered him a weak smile.

"Well, at least I don't have to worry about leaving you by yourself," he breathed. *Have I been holding my breath?*

She smiled a bit wider. "I'm sorry." The smile disappeared.

"Hey," he said, pulling her face into his hands, "cut it the fuck out." He smiled widely and was relieved when she dropped her shoulders, beamed brightly, and began to giggle.

"I kind of kicked his ass."

"He kind of deserved it."

Still, he didn't like the things Jones said.

Note to self: he owes my woman an apology.

When Anthony made his way into the room, Felicity was lying on her back, her hair wild and her eyes fixed on the ceiling. *She's absolutely exquisite.* He gently cleared his throat. She tilted her head down and smiled at him, slowly, sitting up with the blanket wrapped around her. He walked over and placed the plate onto the nightstand and held the orange juice out to her. *She's still staring at me*, and he started to blush. He put his arm out farther to offer her the orange juice. She shook her head.

What's going on?

Anthony sat on the edge of the bed next to her and set the orange juice next to the food, his mind racing. He was confused, but he would not let his face betray him. She let the blanket fall, and she reached out to his face. He reached out to her neck, soft and slender. Something flashed in her eyes, and before he knew it, his mouth was on hers. She was pulling his hair with her left hand and tugging him closer with her right.

You don't have to tell me twice, baby.

UNFINISHED PROJECTS

He would never get enough of this, his white body against her black, peach against brown, ivory and ebony, together, making music with the sounds from their bodies and mouths. She was tempting when she was fully dressed, when she was naked, and when she was in his bed and her hair was a "kinky mess." He didn't care. As long as it was she to whom he got to make endless love at his leisure, he was satisfied.

When they stopped, she looked over to the plate.

"You made me breakfast, Mr. James?" she smiled, taking the rest of the air in his lungs with her.

"Yes, I do believe I did."

"You forgot the fork." She stared at him blankly, and he drew in his breath, not sure what to make of it. Then, she broke into an incredible fit of laughter. He leaned back in disbelief and allowed himself to laugh. *I went through all that preparation, and I forgot the fork. That was stupid, Anthony. But, then again, you were distracted.*

She picked up the plate and began picking at the omelet with her fingers, pulling small pieces and placing them into her mouth. She looked at him every time she did this, and he began focusing on the way her tongue emerged slightly to pull the food into her mouth. Then, she broke off a piece of the omelet and offered it to him. He took it greedily, keeping his eyes on hers and gently nipping her finger.

"Hey," she frowned.

"Tastes like chocolate." *You're incredibly corny, Anthony.*

"You're too corny," she giggled.

"You don't seem to mind."

He wanted this woman to call him names forever. He'd take her verbal abuse any day.

"I want to go get something. Hold on."

She yawned lazily, reaching for her phone. He hadn't realized it was on the nightstand. "Okay, baby love."

After pulling his jeans back on, he stepped hurriedly out of the room, trying to contain his excitement, and made his way toward the shoebox he had hidden in the kitchen. *I'm about to ask this woman to marry me.* He was damn near giddy. He arrived at the box, threw it open, and removed the ring. The big M on the box was betraying. He decided to go with the velvet box within. *She doesn't need to know it's from Mikimoto just yet.* He looked around. He thought he heard something, but he ignored it. *Mimosas and Mikimoto,* he smirked *and my wife.* There was another noise, and it sounded as if someone was calling his name. It was almost imperceptible, small and muffled, but he froze. He held two champagne flutes filled to the brim in one hand and the velvet box in the other.

A soft cry replaced the muffled sound. "Anthony?" It was much clearer now. He dropped the glasses and sprinted into his room, looking for Felicity. She wasn't there. Panic rose quickly as he thought of all the possibilities. Had someone broken in? No, he would have heard that.

"Felicity!"

He heard a loud sob from the bathroom. Without doubt, when he swung open the door, he found her sitting on the cold tiles, her phone in her hand, tears streaming, and her body convulsing. He dropped unceremoniously to the floor, pulling her close to him into his lap, and he cradled her. He wanted to ask what was wrong, but he was too scared. He remembered the box in his hand and shoved it into his pocket, hoping that she wouldn't notice.

He turned his attention immediately back to his love, shaking violently in his lap, her tortured frame curled into the fetal position.

"Felicity?" He'd never dealt with grief. His mother hid it, and his father's eyes never wavered. His brothers took on his father's traits.

Felicity tried to open her mouth and speak, but all that emerged was a wail, and she sobbed again. All she could manage was to hold up the phone. Anthony didn't understand; he took the phone from her seeking answers.

"It's locked," he muttered.

"It's my daddy," Felicity cried. "Someone sent me pictures of my daddy."

Anthony's blood chilled. What type of pictures would set off an episode like this? *Whoever sent the pictures, I will find them and kill them, gladly.* No one messed with his woman, not even his increasingly jealous best friend Jones. He shook the thought out of his mind. Felicity partially regained her composure, took the phone from him, and unlocked it.

As she handed him the phone, she said, "Somebody tried to kill my daddy."

Anthony froze. He was no longer as sure of himself. Did he really want to look at the pictures? At her urging, he looked on the small screen and could make out photos of an elderly man. In spite of the strange device wrapped around his head, the resemblance between the man and the woman crying in his arms was uncanny. He started to move through the photos, without asking, and saw photos of bruises and cuts on his throat. *Jesus, were they going to cut off his head?*

There were countless photos, sent from a blocked number. He couldn't count them, and he didn't want to. His head was spinning as he tried to reconcile the photos and their meaning, her heaving sobs, and what he could possibly do to fix everything.

He thought distantly of Felicity – cool, calm, crazy in bed Felicity – how nothing ever fazed her and how she was always in control of her emotions.

93

UNFINISHED PROJECTS

He thought about how much she loved her father and how much she talked about Louisiana. In that moment, he was glad that his proposal was postponed and glad the ring was safely hidden in his pocket. He had doubts about his ability to protect her from her heartbreaking tears.

She's stopped crying. He looked down at her, and her expression was blank. It appeared that all the color drained from her; she had the look of death on her face.

"Anthony, they beat him," and she was suddenly very serious. She sat up and looked at him. *No, she's looking through me.*

"They cut his throat. That cut was so deep. They beat my daddy. What if my daddy doesn't talk again?" As she said it, her own voice shrunk, and she became incredibly quiet. He already knew that she was returning to her thoughts; he could only hold her closely. *I hope that's not the case. Please, God, don't let that be the case.*

Felicity admitted to Anthony on their third date that he sounded like her father, that his voice was just as powerful, and that it reminded her of home. At the time, he didn't really understand why that was so important.

"I trust you," she offered. "You make me feel safe."

"Safe?" He couldn't imagine why she should feel threatened.

"Yes, safe."

"I don't understand. Did I ever make you feel unsafe?"

She shook her head, shifting her growing hair behind her ear, and she smiled at him, that smile that lit up the room.

"Ant, as long as there's a man in the room, I don't feel safe." She paused, and her smile faded slightly. "I don't feel safe unless you're there." Her smile was gone, and she appeared to go back into her thoughts.

He couldn't believe how serious she was, but he cracked a smile at her. Regardless of how dark her thoughts were, he loved watching her think. He could sit and watch her think forever. The waitress stepped in and brought them both back to earth from their musings.

"Sorry it took so long. Anything to drink?"

"Two shots of gin," Felicity perked up. He stared at her, unbelieving. *I didn't know girls drank gin.* "That's all."

The waitress walked away, wearing the same confused expression he felt form on his face.

"Gin?"

"I'm safe. Let's get loose."

She was back from her universe. Just like that, she'd come back to him.

95

"Felicity, we need to call the police, and we need to get to your father. We need to do this now. We can go and see him together. We can go tonight." The pressing matters at hand came rushing back, and he stated everything as it came to mind.

She ceased crying, but she still sat frozen in his lap, looking through him. He'd spent the last few minutes talking to a statue.

"Felicity, we have to move," he said, reaching for her face.

She pulled away from him and grabbed his hand, her eyes readjusting as she just realized he was there.

"What was in that box?"

Shit.

"Nothing we need to worry about right now. Come on." *So help me, I will carry you out of here.*

A moment later and that's what he was doing, lifting her like a ventriloquist's puppet, her face still frozen, save her eyebrows twitching. He knew that she was trying to drag herself out of her thoughts and away from the pictures. *My poor tortured woman. Her father could be dead right now.* He placed her at the foot of the bed and began to step away when her small hand shot up to his pocket, pulling him closer.

"What is this?"

She still wasn't looking at him. *Jesus, help me through this.* It was taking much effort for him to move on this morning. He'd taken on the stoic traits of his father as he got older, which he learned meant internalizing some things and blatantly ignoring others. Felicity displaying emotions beyond her breadth of control was new to him, but he saw that she wouldn't give this up easily. He got down on one knee, making their eyes level with one another. She was watching him now, her eyes still blank.

"Ms. Woods, I don't think that now is the time but –" He held up a finger to her the second she took the breath to object. "I know my woman doesn't like secrets."

She dropped her shoulders.

We need to be calling 9-1-1 right now. Make it quick, Ant.

"Ms. Felicity Irene Woods, would you do me the honor of being my wife?"

Anthony pulled the box out almost as quickly as he made the offer, his eyes searching hers. He felt this action to be inappropriate; he didn't want her response to be based on raw emotions. He also wanted to call the police, and he wanted to go to Louisiana to see her father all at once. They didn't even know if her father was safe or how long ago the pictures had been taken. As he looked up at Felicity, there were new tears falling now, a crinkle

97

was in the corner of her eyes, and he realized that she was smiling.

"You want to marry me, Anthony? With a Mikimoto ring?"

Shit, how did she know?

"Do you have any idea how lovable you are?"

He offered a sheepish grin. "It really was a lucky guess."

She laughed. *This is so awkward. Her father is on a slab somewhere. Get off of your knee.* He stood, pulling her to her feet by her face. She immediately stopped laughing, clutched his wrists, and the sadness returned to his eyes.

"Don't laugh to keep from crying," he whispered. "You can cry around me."

On cue, the sad tears returned, and she nodded her consent. He kissed her softly and then slowly picked up the phone to dial 9-1-1.

"We're leaving now. Pack a bag."

Chapter 14

The old man was heavier than he expected. It was a slow walk through the hallways to the back of the house. There were so many memories in this house, so many times that he was there laughing with this family.

I will hurt her by hurting him. I don't want to hear from them again. I don't want to see them again. I will make it better. All I have to do is get him back here.

He let the table drop low to the ground with the small latch underneath and placed the groaning gentleman on it. He used the straps on each end, meant for holding logs in place, to keep the man's legs and arms down while he went out to the back and found his bag.

"Jonathan? Jonathan Davis? Is that you?"
Damn, I was trying to hide from him. He swung around, a mock surprise on his face. "Mr. Woods?" His voice was heavy with boyish charm.
"Boy, what you doing in here drowning in this alcohol?"
"Oh, I'm not drowning, Mr. Woods." *Not yet.*
"You mind if I join you, son?"
Yes. "Not at all, sir."

99

UNFINISHED PROJECTS

I wonder if he suspected after I walked him home. It was a spare thought. It was irrelevant what he suspected; he was unconscious. There was a job to do. He pulled down a tool kit from the wall with mallets and screwdrivers.

She was the one who gave him the idea, muttering in the bathroom. "If I could get my hands on that bitch Felicity Woods," her voice trailed off as she spoke. He knew that she was probably getting high again. *I can't get my hands on her*, he frowned. *But I know on whom I can get my hands.* It was a dangerous idea, but there were so many motivations. Jasmine had listed several while she complained about Felicity earlier that evening. It would be easy to find him, but it would be better if the opportunity were to present itself.

He started whistling, pulling out the tools one after another and laying them close to the metal table. *Whistle while you work*, he thought. *Ah, the mallet. I believe he is still sleeping. Maybe we should wake him up. That is an extremely satisfying sound – groans and broken bones. I remember when they trained us to break bones so that we could re-set them.... I don't think I want him to have that opportunity.*

"Leaving you," she scoffed, "to end up with some white man." He wasn't looking at her because he knew that he would probably want to slap her for talking about Felicity that way. He was more interested in what she was saying.

"I wouldn't leave. And then she got the nerve to call up here to ask your advice and then stop calling entirely." She was smoking. He hated her smoke. His smoke was excusable. *Of all the things to hate,* he smirked. She must have thought she was smirking at him, and she continued. *God, this woman never shuts her trap.*

He'd stowed away the tools. He congratulated himself for being creative by using the old man's mallet. *Just in case he starts to remember things about today.* He loved looking at a job well done.

He thought about keeping the mallet and using it on Jasmine when she wouldn't shut up. *You are one violent fucker, Johnny boy.*

Suddenly, he was overwhelmed with sadness for something that he couldn't understand. He started to walk through the house and saw the pictures of that smile that used to send him flying. He was crying. *You don't get to smile.*

"Shut up and leave, Jasmine. I got something to do."

UNFINISHED PROJECTS

Everything she said was sinking in; Felicity hadn't called him in months, and even though he didn't really want to talk to her, he was furious that she was happy with someone else. When she was calling him, it meant she still needed him, and now she didn't.

Jasmine didn't seem to hear him and continued to talk. *Stupid bitch is too high.* Some time ago, he almost lost his job when she showed up asking where he was. She needed money for heroin.

"Jasmine. Get the fuck out of my house."

She looked up, shocked. "Okay, baby."

"I'm not your baby. Get out." *I need to think. I need to think. I need to think.* You shouldn't do this. *Leave me alone!*

Chapter 15

"These Woods sisters are impossible to get hold of, sir."

"Keep calling," the chief growled.

It was a bad day. When Carl first started working, he knew it would be full of bad days. He was on foot more often then, but he turned down promotions. He liked keeping his ear to the street and seeing people he knew. In a smaller part of town, theft was obvious. Fifty dollars missing from an elderly woman an elderly woman meant a sticky-fingered grandchild. However, Mr. Woods being beaten and cut on within an inch of his life was a different story.

Carl fondly remembered Mrs. Woods and their eldest daughter, Mahogany. He best remembered Mahogany. They graduated in the same year, and her mother was their second grade teacher. When she passed suddenly and Mahogany received the news, he was the first person at her side.

"It'll be okay, Mahogany. It will be okay."

She always kept him close, but he knew it was only for friendship even though he wanted much more. He still did. Her younger sisters would joke with him when she wasn't around. "We're going to tell her you like her," Felicity would say as she giggled and then covered her face. Even at five she was adorable. All three of the Woods sisters were enchanting.

"Hey, Green, call from Houston. Some lady with pictures sent to her phone of Mr. Woods."

"Who is it?"

"Lady named Felicity."

"Call them in."

His heart leapt into his throat. *What sick bastard would send pictures like this to anyone?* He wiped the thought out of his mind. *Poor Felicity.*

Chapter 16

"Momma, what's wrong?"

"Nothing honey, Grandpa is just a little sick."

There was no need to lie to her. From the sound of Felicity's voice on the phone, her father could soon be holding hands with death. Still, she wanted her daughter to think of something else on the ride to Louisiana.

"Have you packed your bag yet?" she snapped.

"No," Maxine snapped right back, complete with an eye roll. "Why would I pack a bag if Grandpa has a head cold? You're not being honest Momma."

Mahogany rubbed her temples. *I will not cry in front of this child. I will not beat this child. I will never do either again.*

"You're right, I'm not. But, God help me, I will not let my spoiled child think that she can talk and act any way that she feels when she's been given a direct command. Now, I won't tell you again!"

Chapter 17

The reality was that he needed Felicity more than she needed him.

Jonathan was abandoned at the doorstep of his mother's brown and dark-skinned cousins as an infant. His older cousin, Margaret, only agreed to take him when she found him because she figured it was an obligation worth meeting and that all the mouths she was feeding wouldn't go wanting with just one more at the table. Considering the other circumstances Jonathan could have found himself in, this was a good home where he would eat every night and be dressed every day. His mother, as tortured as she was, wound up in an insane asylum. She would mutter silently to a pillow, willing it to "go to sleep, go to sleep, slumber softly my baby."

The only issue was that Margaret's children and their friends were unspeakably cruel. The worst of the children, an obese and thickheaded monster they referred to as "Big Boy," would taunt Jonathan at any given opportunity.

"You're not a nigger, you know. You're not my cousin. You just live with niggers."

Margaret would admonish him, put him in the corner, and double his chore load, but Big Boy remained the same inexplicably cruel child.

Every now and then, women on the street would look perplexed at the family. Margaret would walk to the grocery store, holding Jonathan's hand. Sometimes the other children trailed along behind, and sometimes it was just the two of them. She liked bringing him to the store because he would remember the grocery list when she couldn't, and she'd let him run ahead of her and pick things up before she got to the aisle. It would cut the trip time in half. The only persons that slowed the dynamic duo were the curious shoppers.

"Margaret, when did you start babysitting?"

"Is that Thomas Davis' child?"

"Whose child *is* that?"

The questions were endless, but most important-ly, they hurt the young and impressionable Jonathan. He would look for his mother in the street in the face of every woman that smiled at him, not knowing what she looked like but hoping that he could prove he was black. He developed a mental picture of his mother as the black Madonna and his being born of her virgin womb and cradled in her arms, having a wide nose and thick wooly hair – all traits opposite to his. He didn't want his mother to have a slim nose like his, to be fair skinned, and to pass for white the way he could. What he didn't understand was that his physical traits were what drove the jealous comments of people like Big Boy. Jonathan's only goal was to show Big Boy that they really were cousins – that they were both black.

In school, he went to sit with the black children in class, but the white children were always much more welcoming.

"Davis, you don't have to sit back there," a young girl with blonde hair would smile. She, like many of the other white children, automatically assumed that he was a white boy. They thought that Ms. Margaret had taken in a foster child because that was the lie their mothers told them as often as they could; even the white women didn't know what to make of him.

"Yeah, Davis," Big Boy would chime in, mimicking the young girl, "It's not like you're a nigger or anything."

At this, Jonathan would turn beet red, and tears would begin to form.

To hide from the stares and protect him from the potential bullying that could erupt from either side of the room, he started sitting behind a boy named Christopher Thomas, whose parents worked as sharecroppers just outside of town. Between the two of them, he found a happy medium. Christopher was white, but his family was considered too poor to play with the other white boys, and Jonathan didn't even know whose he was to make a decision based on race. They got along fine even though Christopher barely spoke.

Margaret's first husband died "in the service of this great country," and she re-married a soldier who lost his wife to a difficult childbirth. He and his distant cousins ended up attending the same school as many ex-military and current servicemen. In spite of some of his cousins learning to love him and treating him considerably better than they had during his younger days, he still felt abandoned by his mother and his race.

"I don't have a family," he'd sulk, confiding only in his cousin Margaret. "People don't leave the ones they love."

"She couldn't take care of you, Johnny boy. Besides, I love you, and I'm not going anywhere." Although his cousin was trying very hard to convince him, Jonathan couldn't understand why his mother would leave.

When he got to seventh grade, he met his salvation.

It wasn't unreasonable to fall for a Woods sister. They were all equally beautiful and black; their blackness was his favorite part. It was palpable, the feel of dark chocolate on your tongue or a muggy night in a bayou. He'd only been smiling and waving at white girls up until middle school because black girls wouldn't give him the time of day. Since no one knew who his parents were and he went unchallenged by the children in the class who didn't really care, he passed easily. But in Felicity, he saw all that he needed.

UNFINISHED PROJECTS

He saw in her his ideal mother, his black Madonna, a woman who was beautiful and strong, a young Nefertiti woman who was revered and feared. She was someone to bow down to, an instant lift to popularity among other black people, and something else he couldn't name. Something carnal came to mind with her, a need to possess her and make her love him, but he dismissed it early on as ardent affection – obsession at the absolute worst – and suppressed all other thoughts from day one.

The attraction was immediate, but the unquenchable love was slow. In seventh grade, he believed that all he wanted or needed was her love and attention. She sat near him, close to the front every day from the start of school. She liked Jonathan because he was quiet and respectful. He would help her carry her books, and he didn't make comments about her skin. She was always fearful that someone would tease her because she didn't look as black as her sisters. Some even went as far to accuse her of having a different father. However, she made it a point to confirm his blackness because he was wildly in love with hers. The other black girls made faces at the two of them while they were in class. One day, close to Thanksgiving, the two of them were working together in a group project, and Big Boy joined with a young Jasmine

Jefferson from the back of the room to torment the two of them.

"So an uppity nigger and a yellow nigger are going to be in a group together? What a perfect match."

"I disagree, completely, Big Boy. Poor yellow thing wasting his good genes on that burnt piece of black they're passing off for a girl. He should be with something fair like me. What would his mother say?"

"What mother?"

"Ha! I almost forgot."

The pair took their time laughing and teetering back in their seats. Jasmine's mean-spirited comments were clearly meant more for Felicity, who was diligently taking notes and apparently ignoring them while Jonathan was burning red.

The teasing lasted all through class. Felicity tried to help Jonathan focus and finish the project, whispering every now and then that he shouldn't think about it. They turned in what she knew would be 'A' work, even if he hadn't paid attention the whole time. In the hallway, Jasmine and Big Boy were still laughing and talking.

"You gonna ignore me, motherless child?" Jasmine guffawed.

Without warning, Felicity shoved her books into Jonathan's waiting arms, put one foot behind Big Boy's and tugged him backward, making him fall awkwardly on the floor, leaving about six inches between her and Jasmine. Then, there was a loud crack that emanated from Felicity backhanding Jasmine who clasped her jaw in shock. Felicity steadied, walked over to Big Boy, bent down and pulled him close to her by his shirt.

"Don't talk about Jonathan that way. If I find out you call him another name or he shows up to school looking even slightly upset, I will knock your teeth in as I almost did missy over there," emphasizing her head nod in Jasmine's direction. Her eyes were narrowed and blazing with anger. Big Boy tried to pull away but nodded quickly so that she would let him go.

She slowly stood up and walked toward the stunned "missy" who was leaning against the doorway, cradling her face in her hands, in shock, and beginning to cry.

"Tears are for suckers," Felicity hissed, "and I just found my first one."

Jasmine's eyes widened in terror, and she looked at Felicity in disbelief, prepared to cower in case she struck again.

"You think you can talk about people anyway you want, Miss Jefferson, and I will allow it as long as you understand that I will make you pay for it every day that you're breathing."

With that, she took back her books from Jonathan who hadn't managed to move and stalked down the hallway. When he shook off the shock, he ran after Felicity, leaving his tormenters silent for the first time ever.

How prescient her comments were, no one would know until years later.

Jonathan would date Felicity all the way to their college graduation from Tulane.

They would break up because he loved her too much and, like his mother, he would lose his mind; he'd find himself broken and abusive, turning to Jasmine as a last resort for his sexual, emotional, and physical frustration. Big Boy ended up in jail before he even graduated from high school.

The memory of that day would drive their actions for the rest of their lives....

Chapter 18

I can't believe this. I'm so incredibly scared. I have never been this scared in my life. I heard bones breaking.

Did he puncture an artery?

Oh, man, I'm coming down already. All this pain is killing me.

I want to open my eyes. I need to get a phone. No one will find me in here. I shouldn't have come here. I shouldn't have gotten so damn high.

He wasn't playing. He told me to go home, and I came back, but it was only because I forgot something here.

That bag... there was a bag full of bloody things. What did he do with that bag? Why did he need it?

He said he had something to do before.

Did he hurt someone?

My eyes feel as if they're sealed shut. I can't open them. My whole arm feels heavy. I can't get to the door. I can't even move.

Shit, Jonathan.

He said something about Mr. Woods. That old dog better stay out of Johnny boy's way today. He called him an old dog. Sad, droopy-faced Mr. Woods better run if my man is coming.

"Get the fuck out of my house!"

114

UNFINISHED PROJECTS

Wait.

"I don't need you here right now! I fucking told you to leave before!"

No.

A resounding crack was heard after a fist hit soft flesh. "I told you not to be here!"

He's been to see the old man already.
Fuck, Jasmine, get off of this floor. All this blood is going to have to get wiped up later. Shit, my legs. I can't feel my legs.
Blood?
Did he break my nose? I mean my neck. Damn it, I'm so high. Get it together.
Cocaine is one hell of a drug. Aha! Chappelle Show. Damn it. This is serious, Jasmine.
Fuck I think he's back.
Shit, Jasmine, you've got yourself in a mess this time.

"Yeah, somebody has been complaining about the smell in here, and the guy that owns it is always yelling. He's a doctor or a surgeon or something... Holy hell, is this woman dead? Hey, David, who is this?"

"Oh, fuck! Call the police!"

UNFINISHED PROJECTS

Open your eyes, Jasmine. You only have to stay awake a little bit longer.

Chapter 19

"Felicity, honey, I need to talk to you."

"What is it, Daddy?"

"I need you to be Daddy's strong girl, okay?"

"What's wrong?" His strong hand almost covered her whole face as he smoothed her wild hair and pushed it behind her ears. She hated being so little in comparison to everyone else. *I can't wait to grow up*. All of her sisters were taller, and they could do more things than she could, especially Mahogany.

"Are we going to see Mommy?"

The tears gathered quickly to his eyes, and he couldn't stop them. He wasn't prepared for the question. *Oh no, don't cry Daddy!*

"We can't see Mommy anymore, honey. Oh, my baby doll!" He hugged the small child tightly, the tears flowing freely, the fear and sadness finally winning over his bravado. Her sisters were sitting in the corner, sobbing quietly, and watching their father explain what even he couldn't understand. Her sister Ebony was holding the toy boat her father made; she brought it in case Felicity tried to break something. Even as a child, she was harsh and destructive. *Are we going to play?*

"Felicity," Mahogany whispered as she walked over and their father put the little girl down, "do you remember when we would go to church and learn about the angels and how they help God watch over us?"

"Uh huh," she said, bobbing her head. "Why?"

"Mommy went to join the angels, bumblebee," Ebony continued while Mahogany gave in to her own sadness. All three of them were standing around her now. None of them could alone answer the child's questions.

No, that's not true. That's not fair.

But she couldn't speak. She was angry, sad, and confused all at once. She knew that her daddy wouldn't lie to her about something like that, but her mommy said that she was just a little sick and that she was going to be fine. They visited her in the hospital last week, and Felicity sang her a song so that she would get better.

"Everything will be fine, honey. Mommy loves you. I really do. I am going to be right here," and she placed her hand over the thumping heart of her six-year old.

With eyes wide-opened, Felicity shot up out of the bed, clutching the sheets, her chest, and Anthony's shirt, attempting to drink in her surroundings. *Breathe, Li. Keep breathing. You're safe. It was just a dream.* The past always caught up to her when she was asleep. She felt scared and vulnerable, and Anthony was nowhere to be found.

"Yeah, I know Jones. I will think about it." His voice echoing around the bathroom in their hotel suite was so reassuring that her breath steadied immediately. They were in Louisiana to bury her father and find her father's killer. She looked around the room in a panic, wondering if there was something she could take to quell the pounding in her chest that continued even though she had calmed down. As Anthony walked into the room, he saw her panicked face.

"Jones, I'll call you back. Yes, damn it. Good bye."

Whether or not Jones finished his thought didn't seem to matter to Anthony at the moment as he slammed the phone down on the dresser. Felicity was glad, for she wanted nothing more than to curl up into his lap in that moment.

"Felicity, what's going on?" He dropped right next to her on the bed, and she immediately took her place in his waiting arms.

"It's nothing, baby. I just had a bad dream." Her whole body was shaking and wet. She'd been sweating and crying in her sleep.

"Another one?" He, himself, might as well have had the nightmare by the way the strain invaded his face. He wrapped his arms around her. "I'm sorry, my darling."

She pulled her legs from under the blanket. It was almost one in the afternoon, and she was still in bed. He was so warm, and she relished the opportunity to sink herself into his arms. Ever since they left Houston, Jones called every day, complaining about the work that wasn't being done while Anthony was away, taking hour after hour of his time away from her. Anthony noticed it, too.

"This dream was different; it was more of a memory. My mom was telling me that she was going to be here," and she gestured toward her heart.

He tilted his head down and kissed her forehead. "I don't doubt that for a second."

"Yeah," she sighed, pulling her body upright, "and now Daddy is there, too."

She felt him becoming tensed. He squeezed her tightly, and she squeezed back.

Anthony met Mr. Woods for the first time when they first got to Louisiana. He and Felicity had run to the hospital after surrendering her phone to someone in forensics at the police station, accompanied by Carl Green and several other officers.

Felicity remembered Carl as though he was a distant memory, and he pinched her cheeks as if she were still the six-year-old girl teasing him about his crush on her oldest sister. She cried on seeing him more for the suppressed memories than the reunion. She was inconsolable after seeing her

120

father. Her sister Mahogany and her niece Maxine being at the hospital only added to her stress.

No one spoke around him. They just sat and watched him expire. Felicity waited with him until he finally gave in, and then she kissed him good night for the last time. It appeared that he waited just long enough to see his girls with the exception of Ebony who had disappeared completely and hadn't answered anyone's calls.

When the absent Ebony came up in conversation, Felicity and Mahogany cast knowing glances at one another. Even Maxine knew a little something and began biting her nails.

"Daddy is going, isn't he?" Felicity asked, an hour before he finally passed. She felt as if she was six once more. Mahogany still looked like her tormented, fifteen-year-old sister, breaking the news of yet another angel.

"The doctors said that what they were doing here was only enough to stabilize him. He'll be gone by the end of the day."

"Damn it," Felicity said as she gave way to another series of shakes and tears. "Where the hell is Ebbs?"

"What did Jones want?"

"Oh," Anthony said. He eased back, looking at her and becoming more tensed. "We got some good news."

She raised an eyebrow. *Don't be reserved now, Anthony Bruce James.*

"Don't do that eyebrow thing at me, lady," and he chuckled, his shoulders dropping and his smile brightening his face. He looked so tired. "We got invited to the Clear Conference."

"Anthony, that's huge!" *Finally we can share some good news.* She thought about a way to keep that smile on his face.

"Ms. Felicity Irene Woods, would you do me the honor of being my wife?"

I recognize that ring. I've seen it before. Is that really a Mikimoto ring? Is he really asking me to marry him? The thoughts racing through her mind were too numerous to organize. She decided to keep it simple.

"You want to marry me, Anthony? With a Mikimoto ring?"

He froze a little bit, looking at her. She wanted to know what was going on in his head, but there was so much more going on. *Daddy. I need to get to my daddy.* "Do you have any idea how lovable you are?"

"It really was a lucky guess."

I know. It's because you know me better than I know myself.

If it wouldn't have been wildly inappropriate, Felicity would have said yes right there with her

122

face covered in tears. She wanted to believe she was finished crying now.

"I know it's a big deal, but I can't go. It's this weekend."

"Oh," she said, visibly deflated. The funeral was this weekend.

"Damn it, Jones knew he would be putting me in an awkward position."

There was a moment of awkward silence. Felicity knew how much the conference meant to him and how important going would be for the company. The Clear Conference was one of the most important things to attend for anyone who claimed to be serious about his ownership of an avionics company like J&J Flight. She wanted Anthony to be more successful than anything in the world, but she also needed him to be with her at the funeral on Saturday. He was her rock now. There was also the slight matter of her sister Ebony still missing in action.

"Go to the conference, Ant. It's really important."

"No, I want to be with you and your family. It's my job to help you through this."

"They'll be around, Anthony. It's okay."

"You said that about your father."

"Damn it, Anthony," and she pushed away from him, glaring at him. "Don't you bring my daddy into this situation, how dare you?"

Felicity was furious and felt her blood boil; how could she be so ready to hurt him when all he wanted to do was be there with her?

"I'm sorry, baby; I didn't mean to say that. I...."

The words escaped him entirely. She relaxed while he tensed, and she knew that both of them were dealing with brand new feelings. She didn't want it to be this way. She eased slowly back over to him.

Felicity took Anthony's face in her hands.

"I know, honey. I'm not angry. That wasn't very nice. I'm not being very nice, either. There's just been so much activity over the past few days, and you've been such a champion for me. It's just that ...." She dropped her head and her hands. *You have to make him understand.* "Anthony, when I was six, I lost my mother. I haven't been raised under a woman's touch, except for Ebbs and Mahogany, and my daddy told me to use my hands for everything. I don't know how to talk, but I know how to think and create. I'm not finished; I'm one of your avionics projects – a new engine with all kinds of promise, but I've been left incomplete."

Felicity became aware that hot tears were falling from her face. She lifted her head and attempted to face him, hoping that she'd be brave enough to meet whatever she found in his eyes. When her eyes finally met his, she saw the tears he'd finally let free, and they were for her.

He's crying for you, Li.

"Please, don't be angry. Neither one of us has anything to be angry about. Just love me and know that I am trying. Come to bed; you look so tired. I want my fiancée to be well rested in the morning before he meets all the important people at the Clear Conference."

Anthony released an audible gasp and reached up, clutching her face in his hands. "Oh, Felicity, my perfect angel. You'll marry me, baby?" The Mississippian in him was dripping from every syllable. *"I'm walking through the Texas sand, but my head's in Mississippi."* The familiar lyric dragged its way through her mind. Now they were both in tears.

"Yes. I will marry you tomorrow in a hefty bag, Anthony. I love you."

"I love you, too. And I'm not going to that damn conference."

She let out a giggle and a smile and found herself in his embrace.

Chapter 20

Mrs. Brown made sure that she shared her love with four people – her husband, her son, Mrs. James, and her son, Anthony. Among the long list of things that made his blood boil, that was the thing that disgusted Jones the most.

In his heart he held nothing but shame and contempt for her ideas and her antics, the fact that he could just barely get her love. She would spoil other people – white people – and he didn't want or understand that; he had anger and a fear of white people from the beginning. His mother would do and say things for white people that he couldn't grasp; he couldn't understand her need to love and follow after them, especially her ignorance and her insistence on his playing with her most prominent client's child.

"I'm nobody's charity case, Momma," he would say, "I'm not gonna be a slave like you."

Mrs. Brown would pause from whatever she was doing – washing someone's laundry or cooking dinner for her growing boy. Her eyebrows would be furrowed and contemplative. She was hurt that he thought that way of her. She would try, again, to make her son understand that the only way in the world she saw was the white way.

"It isn't charity, Jones. You and Anthony are friends. Mrs. James and I were pregnant with you two at the same time. You were raised in the same house – in their house. You're friends. You've always played with him, and you haven't complained until now."

Jones didn't feel as if they were friends. He felt he knew exactly what it was – that his mother was forcing him to get closer to someone for the sake of changing his future. Jones believed he could control his own future. He was grateful for and acknowledged part of his mother's resourcefulness. It was the other part – the part that made him feel like a sycophant, the part that made him think that he would always be under Anthony if he started that way, the part that denied him control – which he disliked.

He would sit there, waiting for his mother to continue, brooding and distressed in a million little ways. Mrs. Brown would finally sigh and end the conversation.

"Jones, you'll thank me for it someday."

Additionally, he hated that name. It was a constant comparison and reminder to and of his father – the 'man' who would show up drunk as he wished, eat, have sex, and leave – and he was reminded constantly that he was "his spitting image;" all of it contributed to his self-loathing. As far as Jones could tell, his father was about as useful as the bald man on the Brawny towels.

When he would search his father's features, looking for a familiar dip in the nose or a slant in the eyes, he found few similarities. He looked at his mother's features for a curve in the lips or the same hair texture. He found nothing. It was at this point that he determined the singularity of his existence – he belonged to no one, looked like no one, and would make it a goal to point this out every chance he got and prove his superiority to Anthony.

Anthony, incidentally, felt entirely different about Jones. He loved having company while his father and older brothers were out fishing. Anthony never wanted to play football and wrestle. He enjoyed reading and making up his own stories. However, he most excelled at inventing. He would produce masterpieces out of scraps such as model planes from pieces of driftwood and old rusty nails. Jones would sit and watch Anthony build and fidget with things all day; it was the one time that he didn't feel any malice for his only friend. It took about three weeks before Jones asked what Anthony was going to do with his creations.

"Do? I guess I will just put them in my room with everything else."

Jones would frown, thinking about his mother having to clean up the mess or tiptoe around Anthony's room so she wouldn't break anything, but he wouldn't object. He hatched a more self-serving plan.

128

UNFINISHED PROJECTS

"I think you should sell it."

It was a small seed that was almost uprooted by Anthony's indifference, but once it was planted, it eventually blossomed into their billion-dollar company.

J&J Flight started with the pair of them selling Anthony's driftwood and makeshift model planes for a dollar a piece. Anthony began to excel in design, using rubber bands and paper clips to motorize propellers on model helicopters and an AKL-26. By the time the two of them were in high school, Anthony developed battery packs and manufactured parts made of real wood and plastic, toiling away for his own pleasure in the garage. Jones developed a show to pitch the airplanes to other students and their classmates' younger siblings. During town fairs, they would stand outside and give demonstrations.

Mrs. James would sit and watch her son, occasionally stepping in to help him paint. She couldn't do much else because Anthony wouldn't let her. Jones turned their airplanes into a major enterprise at school with his marketing schemes, and at every science fair, Anthony won top prize for his creations. The planes started selling at various prices, anywhere from one dollar for a small plane to twenty dollars for a large one. Jones and Anthony's fights decreased, but they fought for entirely separate reasons. Anthony assumed that

UNFINISHED PROJECTS

Jones was angry over the split of the money, the fact that Anthony received the greater share because he was buying all of the parts. The reality was that Jones was jealous and acknowledged that long as Anthony was the one with the brilliant designs, all the business savvy and flashy smiles in the world wouldn't put him on top of the operation.

One night, Anthony was trying to finish an engine he dreamed about the night before when Jones stormed into the garage through the house.

Anthony sighed, heavily. "Hey, Jones-y." He had his back turned to Jones.

"White boy, I can't believe you."

The incredulity in his voice was the only thing that caught Anthony's attention, but he didn't even raise an eyebrow. Jones had started calling him white boy all the time at this point. He carried on with an incredibly small screwdriver on the engine.

"Look at me when I'm talking to you, white boy."

Anthony continued to fiddle.

"I said turn around!" Jones lifted a wrench and threw it at Anthony's back. Anthony didn't even wince because, at the time, he was a much bigger than Jones; it wasn't until college that they became even. However, he finally put the engine down, placed the screwdriver in its proper spot, picked up the wrench and turned around. He thought momentarily about throwing it back at his friend.

"How may I help you, Jones-y?"

What could Jones say? He couldn't be honest about it, about his jealousy and his frustration. He couldn't tell his only friend that he hated his wealth. Could he?

"I... I'm just frustrated."

"Well, I knew that much," Anthony said, lightly, twirling the wrench.

"Sorry."

"Don't be sorry. Talk to me."

Jones didn't want to talk; he wanted to fight. He fought his father and mother to get what he wanted, and now he wanted to fight Anthony to make him understand what was going on. More than anything, Jones was angry that Anthony was still calm.

"Why do you get all the money?"

"I build all the merchandise. And, if I remember correctly, you were the one who called that to my attention when we started."

Jones' dropped his shoulders. They'd made the arrangement during their freshman year of high school when the money was a serious concern and driftwood wasn't enough to satisfy the consumers. He saw himself losing that part of the argument, but he didn't want to back down because then he'd be perceived as irrational.

"I don't think it's fair."

"I don't need the money, Jones."

There it was. That's the thing that was bothering him. He wanted to have Anthony's money because Anthony didn't need it. Anthony seemed to realize the depth of the argument at the same time and took a deep breath, trying to reconcile something he couldn't understand about Jones' life.

Jones was poor. He was undeniably a kid from the other side of the tracks, but he would tell you that in a heartbeat. It was something he was both proud of and angry about at the same time. The airplanes were his ticket to something bigger, to a life like the one Anthony was already living. It was a jealousy of possession, the idea of being the same poor boy forever that made Jones crazy.

Anthony never knew that life. He grew up in a plantation style house that had been in his family for generations. He was purely royal Mississippian, the kind that had Confederate generals on each side and a history of owning slaves. He never looked at Jones as a slave or at Mrs. Brown as anything less than an aunt. He worshipped the ground she walked on and loved her cooking. It took a long time for him to even acknowledge the subtle differences between being black and being white. But Jones saw things differently, and Anthony never had to acknowledge that until now.

He'd never needed to take the time to notice it before.

"Jones, if you want a bigger share, then say so. My mom will buy the materials. Just don't get angry with me for something you can't articulate and that I can't fix."

Jones sighed heavily. Why was Anthony always able to take the higher road? Why was he so perceptive? It wasn't fair. He wasn't going to get his wish to beat Anthony black and blue – especially black.

"How about fifty-fifty?" Jones knew it was time to give up.

"Fifty-five, forty-five plus ten percent of all earnings at the end of the year?"

Damn it, white boy. It was a smarter deal and more reasonable than Jones could think of, and he knew that all of Anthony's money was going into making a better product. He idly thought that Anthony could be a businessman if he wanted.

"Okay," he resigned. Jones was tired and needed to go home. He needed to think. In a year, the two of them would be headed to college – Anthony was looking at Ole Miss, and Jones was content with Jackson State, thinking Old Miss was out of his reach. Shortly thereafter, they would be college graduates. He knew that he would have to stick by Anthony if he wanted to get anywhere and that they both wanted to keep the business going.

The business would be his ticket out of Mississippi, at the very least.

"Jones, get some sleep and come back here when you're ready to get creative for the fair tomorrow."

Anthony walked over and clapped Jones on the shoulder. He was glad the argument was over, glad that they could come to a halt on the disagreement even if it was another temporary arrangement.

"Shake on it?"

"Of course."

They shook and parted ways, Anthony offering a weak smile and Jones, a smirk.

"So, you're going to marry her?" Jones couldn't hide the hurt in his voice. He'd tried for so long to separate them. It was easily the most tiring four months of his life. Now, not only was Anthony not coming to the IEEE/AIAA conference, which was a week after the Clear Conference that he skipped, but he was also going to marry somebody's secretary. At least his old friend had the courtesy to come to the office and say it to his face.

"You know she's bringing nothing but her ass to the table, right? It's not a good deal, Anthony."

"Damn it, Jones, this isn't about business."

"Then what the hell is it about? I want you to make me understand because all I know is that my boy is going down the aisle with some girl who cracked in his best friend's face."

134

Anthony chuckled at the memory of Felicity's rage and his amusement at Jones' grudge.

"I don't think it's fucking funny, white boy."

"I think your being this possessive and childish at thirty is very funny, Jones. And you need to stop calling me white boy. I have a name so use it."

Jones inhaled suddenly. Anthony sounded and looked almost murderous from the other side of the table, and Jones wasn't prepared for that aspect of his friend.

"Fine, *Anthony*," he said, not bothering to hide his disgust with his friend. "I hope you know what you're getting yourself into."

Jones was furious, but he couldn't read Anthony's emotions. It was something at which Anthony excelled; he could sit still as a statue with a blank face for as long as he saw fit. He sat there, expressionless, looking away from Jones and thinking. Were they still friends?

"You know, Jones. I've been thinking about some things. I've been thinking about whether or not we should continue this partnership and whether or not you and I should even be associates."

"What the hell –"

"I'm not finished, Jones."

Jones waited with bated breath. *What the fuck is he talking about?*

"You openly insult my fiancée, make passes at her, and berate me for not being a selfish ass like yourself. And that's just the tip of the iceberg."

Jones felt his jaw drop open. Anthony was facing Jones with his eyes blazing, taking him head on now with no restraint.

"Our entire lives, I've been helping you, feeling as if I was paying you back for something your mother didn't do or your father didn't – hell, I don't even think you know at whom you're angry. I helped you build this company, and we both cherish this place. I'm the reason we even have this place, the reason we can both live our lives this way. I fought you as a kid, and I helped you manage your money – I've been holding your damn hand for years."

Jones was barely able to keep his composure. When Anthony spoke honestly about how he felt, it was a new sensation and entirely too much for him.

"I'm sick and tired of this game that we keep playing, Jones. So, I'm going to give you an ultimatum. If you can't keep it together and learn to keep your mouth shut, then I will treat you like the second-rate businessman you are. If you want to whine and act like a brat, you have that luxury, but understand that you will be whining all the way home to Mississippi because you won't have the luxury of the company apartment in Houston."

UNFINISHED PROJECTS

Jones turned to ash. His mouth went completely dry. He couldn't understand what he was being told.

"Are you telling me... are you saying that I'm fired?"

"If you keep running off at the mouth then, yes. That's exactly what I'm saying."

Jones sat back in his chair, covered his face with his hands, and then leaned forward and supported himself on his elbows at the edge of the table.

"Everything will be gone, Jones. I'm taking your name off the warehouse and everything. I might just leave you here to run an empty building by yourself because all the patents, all my designs, they leave, too."

"This is blackmail."

"No, this is you growing the fuck up."

Jones shook his head.

"I'm in love, Jones. I'm madly in love. For the first time since we were kids building model planes out of sticks, I'm in love. You don't understand it because you've been too selfish to let yourself feel. You've been stuck on going to conferences, parading around in your suits and smiling in people's faces, and grabbing girls. You keep trying to keep me to yourself, but you do everything in your power to show me just how much you can't stand the sight of me."

"You make it sound as if we're in a relationship."

"This is a relationship!"

Jones looked up.

"You're my best friend and that's not saying much. You've got to let this go, damn it. Damn you, Jones. You make this so fucking hard. We're supposed to be friends."

"We're still friends?" Jones felt his spirits lift in spite of himself. Anthony was the same unrelenting optimist, willing to see the good in everyone, but Jones knew now that he'd been taking advantage of the same trait that was saving his ass now for years. *Maybe... maybe we really were friends this whole time.*

"Unless you'd rather have a different arrangement. But you also need to apologize to the future Mrs. James."

Jones took a deep breath. Apologizing was a difficult task. It required more effort than Jones cared to exert at the moment, and it meant the possibility of the apology going unaccepted. He'd acted like an ass and he knew that. Admitting it would be the hurdle.

"I will try."

Anthony seemed to look relieved.

"Okay, good. She's outside."

"Wait, what, now?"

"Yes, now. Honestly, it's a shame I have to threaten to dissolve our company for you to get off your ass."

He was going to dissolve the company?

"You wouldn't."

"Oh, but I would. You know damn well I wouldn't be able to make the deals without you – "

"And I wouldn't be able to make the planes without you."

Anthony smiled.

"A deal, Jones. Fifty-fifty?"

Jones' face split in half with a smile. He couldn't believe his ears.

"Shake on it."

The two of them emerged from the office, Anthony's arm around Jones' shoulder. He really was absurdly tall; Jones looked and felt like a younger brother under Anthony's weight. This feeling was intensified when Anthony gave him a firm pat on the back and pushed him toward the waiting Felicity.

Damn, she really is gorgeous. If I can't have her then... Anthony is the man for the job.

"Hello, Jones." *Cold as ice, though.*

"Felicity. I'd like...."

She raised her eyebrow at him, and he immediately felt small. She was going to make it difficult. "First of all, I'd like it if you wiped that look off your face. I'm trying to apologize here."

Her face fell immediately, and she glanced quickly at Anthony.

"No, Ant isn't going to stop me from talking to you like this. This is how I talk. Now pay attention."

She paused and smirked. Either he was amusing her, or she was making fun of him. He decided on the former.

"Okay, here it goes," and he bent down to both knees. *If the lady wants comedy, that's just what I will give her.* Her shocked face and Anthony's gasp let him know that he achieved the desired effect.

"I'm an ass, and I've always been one. My best friend has been dealing with it for thirty years, and God has been dealing with it for nine extra months. I know that now. It took thirty years for that to get through my skull. What I'd like to say to you is I apologize. I'm sorry that you got the short end of the stick, and I'm sorry that I made passes at you and insulted you. Your kicking my ass in public was sobering, and I see that my best friend really is in love with you." He paused and then bowed into the carpet at her feet. "I humbly beg for your forgiveness."

"What?"

He tilted his head up slightly.

"I humbly beg for your forgiveness?"

She started giggling, and her giggling gave way to a relentless laughter that came from both her and Anthony.

"I can't believe you just did that, Jones."

Felicity smiled. "He certainly is a character."

140

"Can I get up off the floor now?"

Felicity laughed again. "Yes, Jones, please do. I think your secretary thinks something is wrong with you. Prostrating yourself must be a new feature."

At that, Jones shot up to his feet and grabbed Felicity before she could object, squeezing her into a tight hug. "Please forgive me." *Wow, this feels... new.*

Through strained lungs, Felicity managed to say, "You're forgiven," and he put her down immediately. He felt liberated; he had back his best friend, and the girl that publicly embarrassed him forgave him for a lifetime of reproachable behaviors.

"Now," he smiled, "let's celebrate! Danielle, I'm going to need some champagne."

Since he was now in the business of apologizing, he thought he would give Melody a call. Perchance, he could make amends with another important woman that day. When Anthony and Felicity left the office, he locked the door to his office and dialed Melody's cell phone.

"Hello, Jones." She was upset with him, but there was a hint of anticipation in her voice. "How may I help you today? Another thirty minute session, perhaps?"

"Melody, I'd like to say something."

"Well, don't let me stop you from anything important."

"Melody, I apologize."

She was silent on the other line. He thought he heard her gasp in surprise, and it wouldn't be outlandish if she had. He'd treated her horribly.

"If you're still on the line," he continued, disregarding the silence, "I'd like to take you out to dinner tonight; we can go anywhere you want. But I'd like to sit down and speak with you."

He could make out the faint pattern of her breathing on the other line.

"Um, Jones, are you sick?"

He laughed at her. *Damn, I must be an ass.*

"Are you available for dinner tonight?"

Chapter 21

His name was Zebedee, Zebedee Biggs. He was born to Everson and Jane Biggs, and they owned the most spacious house in Shreveport.

He started playing football as a child, taking after his father in every way. He made winning plays and earned MVP every season. People referred to him as Biggs; big is what he was and big is what he became – a big deal, a big man, and member of a big family involved in big business. He never asked what his father did for a living, and it was largely because it didn't matter. He and his twin sisters, Samantha and Sarah, were spoiled in ways that would make jealous the Queen of England. They wanted for nothing but a better father.

When the twins were born, Everson struggled with his new responsibilities. He didn't enjoy the prospect of sharing his wife with God, let alone two newborns. He was extremely possessive when they met – "It's because I don't want anyone to look at you but me" – and she was fine with it. Everson Biggs was the cutest man in town, and it didn't make sense for her to pass up the opportunity to be seen with him. She fell for him hard and had to learn what being seen with him would mean the hard way.

Everson bought Jane new things, expensive jewelry, new clothing, and a house on the Mississippi before they were married. He lured the unsuspecting country girl in under the guise of adoration when, in fact, he saw the opportunity to rule her.

"Good," his father said, "get one that will obey, and you won't be like me." His father married three times and finally gave up. Aside from Everson, there was only one other Biggs relative – his loose and distant cousin Lela who always seemed to be pregnant. But Everson wasn't supposed to know about her, and he knew better than to allude to her.

When he finally married Jane, it was clear that she worshipped the ground on which he walked. He could have murdered her whole family, and she'd argue that he was innocent. The woman was mesmerized.

Two nights after carrying her over the threshold, he hit her in the arm for dropping a new vase. "Does your arm not work? Is your hand malfunctioning? The woman that I married is perfect; get it together!"

By the time Zebedee was five years old, his father's antics had given way to full-blown alcoholism and abuse. Zebedee and his sisters seemed to be immune and mostly ignored, but their foolish mother endured Everson's wrath. Jane should have run far away from Everson. His twin sisters would sulk from time to time over their ailing mother when their father was out, but young Zebedee was never interested in staying in the house to hear his mother's distressed cries for God's help. He stopped believing there was a God; how could God let his mother be treated in such a fashion?

Everson imparted to Biggs the same philosophies and pearls of wisdom his father gave him. "Zebedee, you remember that a woman who isn't obedient is a woman you can't trust. She'll leave you and she'll hurt you. She'll raise your children to be just as stubborn and disobedient as she is. You have to have control, son." Everson would pat his boy on the head and smile to himself, assured that he'd done a good deed and given a good speech in spite of his apparent inebriation. "You go on to bed, son."

As Zebedee got older and became known as Biggs, his father let him in on more secrets. "Did you know," he'd lean in conspiratorially, "that hitting your mother makes her feel everything more when we do the nasty?"

Biggs was disgusted and confused. He'd already taken three girls' virginity as a sophomore in high school and had sex with several more, all of whom seemed to feel plenty, but he refrained from commenting. His father was barely standing, filled to the brim with drink.

"It makes her more sensitive; she likes it more." Biggs thought his father was wrong, and he felt as if it would be awkward to hit someone during sex.

However, on one occasion he spanked a girl, and she started giggling about it. He stored the sadistic idea in the back of his mind because he really didn't like hitting women. It felt too much like something his father would do to get control, and he didn't want to end up like his father, did he?

When Biggs came back from college – after his father passed and his mother was sent to a nursing home – he took a visit to the high school, following a lead his sisters gave him for a long lost cousin. They stressed the importance of staying in touch with family, something he had no interest in. Students were leaving from school, and he was straining to find a familiar face, looking for a telling blonde streak of hair. Instead, he found a face that left him speechless. Ebony Woods was emerging from the school with another younger girl trotting along beside, her sister he assumed, and to Biggs, she was incredible. He was certain of two things: she had a smile that would champion Miss America's and a body to go with it. All he had to do was find out her name.

Biggs' staring hadn't gone unnoticed by Ebony or Felicity, and Mahogany noticed it when she approached as well. Mahogany was picking up her younger sisters, watching the awestruck Biggs standing at the gate. Without preface, Mahogany shouted, "Pictures last longer, pervert!" and grabbed her two sisters, pulling them out of sight.

146

Felicity got free and trotted alongside Mahogany without protest; Ebony wistfully looked back.

"Let me go, Mahogany," she whispered.

"What? No. That man looks like five types of trouble. He's practically my age. Standing there, gaping at you as if you were on display; he ought to be ashamed of himself. I have to go pack for Atlanta!"

"Mahogany, let go of me, or I will punch you in the face" Ebony threatened.

Whether it was out of shock or resignation, Ebony didn't know, but her sister dropped her wrist and stood, waiting. "Well, Ebony. What's your master plan? Don't take forever; I need to be ready to leave for next week!"

Ebony didn't need one. Biggs was already walking toward her.

Biggs met Jasmine, his not-so-distant cousin Lela's daughter, by accident shortly after he started dating Ebony. He recognized the facial features and the blonde streaks of hair flailing in the wind. From afar, she could pass for one of his sisters. They had their first familial introduction the night Ebony and her sisters beat her down. Biggs broke up the fight, pushing away Ebony while Felicity was grabbed by her boyfriend Jonathan. Mahogany stood, arrested in motion on the sidewalk; she was visiting her sisters for the weekend.

147

"Jesus, Ebony, you almost killed her. She is just a little girl."

"Yeah, well, she had it coming." He'd never seen her so furious.

"Stay over here. I'm going to ask if she's all right."

"Why?" She was visibly upset by his concern for her.

"Don't worry about it. Just stay put."

Biggs walked over, ignoring Ebony's cussing and swearing and demands that he come back, and pulled Jasmine to her feet. As he looked into her eyes, there were the salient signs – the fair skin, the eyes that never seemed to be one color, the downward slant of the eyebrows, and the blonde hairs. He couldn't believe it – he'd been trying to avoid this day – but he wasn't keen on a family reunion. One look at Jasmine and he knew all he needed to know.

"You okay, Miss Jefferson?"

"Why are you helping me?" She yanked her arm away from him. She didn't want to be touched.

"I was just trying to help you out," he said, throwing his hands up in defense. *After all, you're my cousin.*

She glared at him, and he thought the better of a family reunion once more. He would tell his sister about it later, if he bothered to remember. For the time being, he wanted to calm his increasingly furious girlfriend.

148

"If you want to help her, then stay over there!" she'd shouted at him.

"Stop it, Ebony," he breathed, grabbing her by the arms and staring into her eyes. Her hair was wild, and all he could think of as she gave way and leaned into him was the master taming the beast at a circus.

Ebony and Biggs had been dating around seven months when she learned she was pregnant. She'd just graduated from high school, and Biggs ended up graduating a semester early. She didn't want to focus on her pregnancy because she didn't want it to be true. She was rightfully worried about his response, about the fact that she didn't even have a plan for the future, and about whether or not he loved her the way that she loved him. In many ways, Ebony was just as hopelessly in love as Jane and who could blame her? Zebedee Biggs was an all-star in every way, an object to be sought after and possessed in the same way as his father Everson was. He had everything he wanted and more for the woman of his choosing. At the time, that woman was Ebony Woods, so she bravely assumed her role.

"Biggs, we need to talk," she said. They were in his car outside of her house cuddled in the backseat.

"Yes, we do," he sighed. He knew Ebony was pregnant before she did. Her body was changing in little ways, but he watched over her so much that

149

he knew when her period was coming before she did.

"We do?"

"Ebbs, you're pregnant. I know."

She gasped, looking up at him in disbelief. "How did you know? How did you find out? Who told you?" No one could have told him. She hadn't even told her sisters.

"You know I know you inside and out, crazy girl."

She relaxed and giggled a little. "This is very true, crazy man."

"Big man," he corrected her, laying her body out along the back seat, leveling himself over her by resting his hands on either side of her face. He was happy there was so much room in his new car.

"My big man."

He dipped down – his old football coach would call it a perfect push-up – and kissed her. "I have good news, too."

"My being pregnant is good news?" she asked him, all of the confusion sending her eyebrow into a twitch.

"Absolutely," he assured her, "especially since I've been promoted to senior marketing rep."

She squealed in delight. "Biggs, that's huge!" She pulled him into her, hugging him tightly. "I love you so much! I'm so proud of you."

He would have preferred they stay forever in that happy moment. He loved his wife in ways that she didn't understand, but, as their happy family expanded, he got angry about trivial things. He thought the children were supposed to bring the family together, but Ebony and he drifted further apart. He was angry when she behaved like his mother and angry when she didn't. He liked the way she reacted to rough sex and how fragile she was after he beat her to a pulp. He couldn't reconcile one version of himself with the other – the version his father would champion and the version that loved his wife.

After they broke the news of Ebony's pregnancy to the family at large, the reactions varied. Mr. Woods gave him a death grip and demanded a wedding take place within the next two weeks. "My daughter is not going to be paraded as a ruined woman, young man." Biggs couldn't feel his hand for about three hours afterward but was happy Mr. Woods didn't threaten to kill him. His mother, Jane, on the other hand, objected to the entire affair and nearly lost her mind. "I've never met this young woman, and I am absolutely certain she is only after your money. You are entirely too trusting, Zebedee, and it is clear to me that this little hussy just wants to get into this family to shame our good name." Biggs didn't feel like reminding his mother of her entire marriage and the shame and embarrassment she brought upon herself or of the way his sisters were carrying on with rather dangerous characters in Chicago. He also didn't think that she understood his intentions; he wasn't at the nursing home to ask permission. It was an informative trip, only.

The small wedding occurred within a week of the announcement, and seven short months later, Ebony gave birth to Phoebe Biggs. He was extremely fond of his baby girl, every bit a Biggs' child; she had blonde hairs and eyes that glistened hazel and light brown and sometimes a shade of blue. He spoiled his girl just as his father did, and she wanted for nothing. Following shortly after her were the sons, each coming in rapid succession; every time he turned around, Ebony was pregnant again. He knew part of that was his fault since he released every frustration on his wife's body. After Phoebe's birth was Gregory's and Zacharias' followed by Dennis' and Teresa's, which came last with less than a year's time between them.

By the time Zacharias was born, Biggs began losing his temper over the smallest things. Everything was Ebony's fault. "Did you forget to feed my child? Is that why he's crying?" he would yell, or "You need to clean up these diapers and take care of this mess. I'm not here to clean up after these children during the day, and I shouldn't have to come home to their mess."

Ebony's only release from her husband's rages was party planning. It would distract him from crushing her ribs or bruising her back. All of her children had the most spectacular birthday parties, and so did Biggs. Christmas was always fabulous in their home – perfectly trimmed trees and presents that looked as if they belonged at a Macy's floorshow. The food was always ornate – garnished and colorful, straight off the cover of *Better Home and Gardens* with matching silverware and place settings to boot. If Ebony had the choice, she'd be in the business of interior decorating and party planning, but Biggs was adamant about not letting her work. "I take care of you," he would say. "That's my job."

On Ebony's birthday, she'd bake a single cupcake and place a candle in it. She'd light it, close her eyes and, if she managed not to cry, she'd make a wish, blowing the candle out and sighing in desperation.

She let Biggs force himself onto her when she thought it was time for another child. She was grateful that she could at least anticipate his rages and that he wasn't a drunk the way he admitted his father had been. She was pleased that for the nine months she was pregnant and a few months following that she was invincible and he was sweet again. Her sisters would always hear little breaks in her voice when they got on the phone with her. "Ebony Marie Woods, you are lying to yourself if you think you're going to pull the wool over my eyes," Mahogany would begin in a manner that was harsh and angry, and then she would end sweetly with

153

UNFINISHED PROJECTS

"Please tell me what's wrong little sister." Ebony didn't know how to respond, especially during the time when Mahogany was learning how to care for Maxine. Maxine and Phoebe were the same age.

"I don't know what's wrong. I don't think anything is wrong," she'd added quickly if Biggs was walking into the house.

"Ebbs, you're lying. He's hitting you isn't he? I should kill that little shit." The ever-militant Felicity would always be prepared to march in and hurt someone. She wondered, idly, whether or not Felicity would ever learn to control her temper.

"No, Felicity. Don't kill anybody." She would smile weakly and hurry to get off the phone.

Biggs was painfully aware of the fact that his children were terrified of him and that his wife no longer looked at him with love. He would try to make it up by spending money on trips, taking time off from work, and adorning them in expensive clothes. But Ebony got smaller and smaller; she could fit in a size zero at one point.

Young Phoebe was aware that her father was doing more harm than good. She would warn her siblings in little ways to stay out of the way and explain that their father was sometimes a mean man. The boys didn't always agree with Phoebe, but they learned better the night that their father came home and tossed Gregory out of the way to get to the petrified Ebony.

UNFINISHED PROJECTS

"No, Biggs, don't!" She watched Gregory land with a hard thump.

Phoebe ran in and pulled Gregory's crumpled form back into her room where she cowered with her siblings.

"You're telling me what to do now? I own you!"

That night, when Biggs put his hands on Gregory, Ebony knew it was time to go.

Chapter 22

"Thanks for coming to see me, Carl," Mahogany sighed. "I've been trapped in the house trying to take care of Felicity and Ebony all day."

A young Carl Green sat down at the table, ready to help Mahogany with her homework. He'd do anything for Mahogany Woods. When they met in grade school, Mahogany was the prettiest girl in her mother's class; anyone could attest to her beauty, and it wasn't just to get an 'A' from the teacher. Mrs. Elaine Woods saw that Carl was smitten, but she knew her daughter Mahogany wouldn't be an easy prize, even at her young age. Second grade would set the pace for the rest of grade school, junior high, and high school. Mahogany was endowed with an incredible figure. Carl knew that other boys liked her for the physical characteristics, but he appreciated her mind, a mind to which he only had access. She was clever and street smart. She knew how to take care of herself and her sisters.

When Mrs. Woods passed away, Carl admired her courage and the way that she supported her father and the rest of the family by babysitting and buying new clothes for her sisters. Mahogany made everyone attend church on Sunday, and she cooked breakfast and dinner out of almost nothing. She assumed the role as woman of the house.

UNFINISHED PROJECTS

Mahogany needed Carl the way she needed oxygen. He was her best friend and the keeper of all her secrets. She was acutely aware that she was his best friend as well. He didn't socialize with anyone but her, and he would have been a loner if they hadn't been friends in grade school. For a long time, she was afraid that he was gay, but it wasn't because she had designs to date him. She didn't want him to be gay because she knew that he would be an incredible man to fall in love with for some lucky woman.

"Carl? Is that you?"
My God, she is still gorgeous. "Mahogany." *Please, floor, stay under me today.*

All through high school, Carl made it a point to be in every single one of Mahogany's classes. He chased after her like a puppy, carrying her books and walking her home, but his behaviors were largely unnoticed by the other high school students. Carl had been working at Mahogany's whims since second grade.

Senior prom was their undoing. Naturally, they attended the prom together. Carl's father loaned him a tuxedo, and Mahogany wore a self-altered dress of her mother's. She saved the money for some new shoes for her sisters – *admirable as ever.* In Carl's mind, this was just as good as a first date, but there was work to do. Three weeks after the prom, he was going to basic training for the army; he intended to try his luck and follow in his father's footsteps. He intended to ask Mahogany to marry him.

Ebony was fourteen and Felicity was nine when Carl made the decision to ask for Mahogany's hand in marriage. He'd already been to see her father, and although Mr. John T. Woods was one of the hardest men to convince of anything, he had received full permission.

Mr. Woods was protective of his girls and knew that they could control the world with one of their smiles. His angels were reserved for only extraordinary men, and he saw this characteristic in Carl.

After the DJ announced that there would be one slow dance before the night was over, Carl escorted Mahogany onto the floor. They'd been laughing and enjoying one another's company all night. Mahogany ignored the stares of all the boys; her dress fit like a glove, and the fabric seemed to cling to her skin in a way that showed appreciation for her existence. She was stunning; she always had been. Carl was just waiting for the opportunity to say so.

"It's been such a long time." Mahogany started to cry in spite of herself. She came to the hospital as soon as Felicity called to tell her what happened. She was tired from the drive but glad to be there. Her father was a crumpled mess in the other room, but her best friend was here to take care of her again.

"Oh, Mahogany, come here." Carl opened his arms to her. That's where she belonged. It was a place she never should have left.

Carl pulled Mahogany into the middle of the dance floor and bowed graciously. Mahogany couldn't help but think of Carl as dapper, even if it was his father's tuxedo. She loved her best friend for always being there for her. He pulled her in close, and she felt herself give in to his warm embrace. She knew that he liked her, and she wanted to like him, but try as she might, it wasn't in her. Deep down, there was a pang, and the idea of losing him scared her. She leaned her head on his shoulders and rested entirely in his arms.

"I missed holding you, Mahogany. I missed keeping you safe."

"I missed you, too."

Maxine looked on at her mother. She was so happy to see her in this way, the way she imagined that she always should have been – wrapped up in the arms of a man who loved her.

"Are you tired?" Carl whispered.

"Yes. Dancing away the night," Mahogany said as she looked up at him and smiled broadly. Her hair was pinned up, and she reminded him of a princess.

"I could never tire of seeing that smile, Mahogany."

"Well, I should hope you'd be used to it by now, Carl." She giggled.

"I guess you're right," he breathed. He was getting more and more nervous. "There's something I'd like to ask you Miss Woods."

His face was suddenly serious. She didn't know what to think of him at that moment. A thought crossed her mind, but she dismissed it. *Surely he wouldn't ask me that.*

Carl knelt down at her feet and she gasped, covering her mouth with her hands, her eyes wide in terror. *Oh my God, he would ask me that.*

"Carl, this is my daughter Maxine. Maxi, this is Mr. Green."

She has a daughter but no ring? Oh, Mahogany, who could ever leave you?

"Hi, Mr. Green."

"Hi, Maxine. My, you're just as gorgeous as your mother."

The young lady smiled herself silly. "Thank you, Mr. Green."

"You can call me Carl."

160

Mahogany watched him pull out a small green box, still in disbelief. He looked up at her, his eyes almost as wide as hers. He was terrified.

"Carl, what are you doing?" she finally managed to ask. "Get off the floor," she hissed. He ignored her.

"Mahogany Elaine Woods, I've been in love with you since I met you in second grade." The words were spilling out of his mouth, and he couldn't believe that the floor hadn't opened up beneath him. He was asking the woman of his dreams to marry him. "Would you do me the honor of being my wife?"

"Oh, Carl," she was crying. She couldn't believe he'd asked this. Everyone on the dance floor stopped and waited, frozen in the moment with them. The DJ stopped playing his music and stared, sharing in the anticipation.

When Carl took them to see Mr. Woods, he was worse than before. The old man started to cry when he watched Mahogany slip into the room behind Carl and even more when his granddaughter appeared behind his daughter. Maxine started to look like Mahogany in little ways. They had the same mannerisms. Although he never received the full story from Mahogany about her pregnancy, he was proud of her and the way that she took care of

Maxine. He'd been proud of her since she was fifteen. As he cried, Mahogany and Maxine rushed to his sides, holding his arms and gently kissing his face.

"Please don't leave us, Daddy."

But the old man was weak and barely had his eyes open to see them. By the time Felicity arrived to meet them, he was ready to be read his final rights.

"Carl," Mahogany implored, "please get off the floor."

Before he could object, she reached down and pulled him to his feet. He was stuttering something she couldn't understand, and he was in tears. *Why is she taking me outside?* She walked, leading him out of the dance and into the hall.

"Mahogany, I don't understand."

"No, Carl, you don't. I can't believe you just did that." She felt the blood rush to her face, and her eyes began to swell with tears of frustration. "Why would you do that in front of all those people? I probably look like a monster now!"

"Stop it, Mahogany. What are you talking about?"

"My answer is no, Carl. I can't marry you." She spluttered the last part in disbelief, shocked that he would even think that way. *Did I say I want to get married? We aren't even dating!*

Her response to him was a shock that sent his head reeling. She'd said no but why? Was there something he had missed? *I don't understand.*

"Carl, I've never thought of you as anything more than a friend. You're my very best friend. What would make you think that I would do anything to jeopardize that?"

"Mahogany, I just...."

"I can't believe this, Carl."

He couldn't believe it either. She looked at him, tears trickling down her face.

"I'm going home now."

"No, Mahogany, please. At least let me take you home."

She pouted and started to protest, thinking that he would try to change her mind when they were alone, but she knew that it would be worse if her father discovered that he let her go home alone. *Did he even ask my dad?*

"Fine, but I'm sitting in the back seat."

"Mahogany," he started. Time made him much braver. Over the week that Mr. Woods rested in the hospital waiting to expire, Carl Green discussed sundry things. He talked about how if Mahogany were to show up again, he would ask again. Mr. Woods willingly gave his permission. He wanted to tell Carl what he was thinking – that Mahogany needed him just as badly as he still needed her.

163

UNFINISHED PROJECTS

She'd been there for two days, and Carl knew that it was now or never.

"Thanks for driving me home." She got out of the car and slammed the door before Carl could even respond. There was an icy silence between the two of them the whole ride. His bitter tears poured freely as he drove himself home.

When Mahogany got inside, she ran crying to her room and sobbed, head stuck in her pillow. It wasn't the way she wanted the night to end, but she temporarily mused that she didn't want to talk to Carl Green ever again. Ebony and Felicity came in and helped their sister get changed into her pajamas; they lay in bed with her until she fell asleep. When Carl arrived at home, he sat up letting the television watch him through the night, crying silently and staring into space.

"I know it's been a long time. We haven't seen one another in years, and I'm sorry I ever let that happen. You're here with this beautiful child, and I can't believe I missed that. I want nothing more than to be a part of your life. I want to share life with you. You're the only woman I ever loved."

Carl dropped to one knee and produced the same small green box and opened it. Inside, was his mother's wedding band, in the same perfect condition as when she first wore it.

"I've asked this question once before, but this time, your father won't let me take no for an answer." He paused, looking at Mr. Woods who gave a small nod. "Mahogany Elaine Woods and um... Maxine," he grinned, nervously, "will you let me be the man of the house, a husband, and a father? Mahogany, will you marry me?"

"Carl," Mahogany started, breathless and filled to the brim with love so tightly that she could have burst to pieces. "I – "

"Yes!" Maxine shouted. Everyone in the room stopped and looked at her, including Mr. Woods. "What? He asked me, too," she added sheepishly.

Mahogany smiled adoringly at her daughter and then looked back at her father, love and tears brimming in their eyes. "Thank you, Daddy," she mouthed. The old man gave another nod; he was so incredibly weak.

"Carl," she smiled majestically, "I think it's high time I said yes."

Chapter 23

"Well, Miss Jefferson, you've made incredible progress over the past three days. I'm happy to say that you're almost completely healed."

The doctor was standing in front of Jasmine, smiling and very pleased for good reasons. When she first arrived at the ER, she was in a dire condition with three broken ribs, a broken nose, contusions on her arms, and a severe concussion. She was also under the influence of several different controlled substances including heroin.

"We've successfully pushed most of the drugs out of your system, and we have been giving you a new IV every few hours to help your dehydration problem. You will be expected to attend rehab to avoid and assist with any relapses. We also gave you some penicillin to get rid of whatever might have been injected or forced into you while you were unconscious since there were several fresh injection marks on your body." Here, he paused and frowned, looking at his chart and trying to avoid her eyes. "There's just one more thing you need to know." He dropped his voice to a whisper and closed his eyes. He'd have to look her in the face for this one. This was his least favorite part of every visit.

Jasmine held her breath, trying to process everything. She wasn't aware she'd been injected with anything she hadn't purchased. She didn't even remember the substance on which she was high. All she remembered was sniffing a little cocaine. She did know that if she'd been brought to the hospital higher than a kite, she'd probably have to do some time outside of rehab. Maybe they'd have mercy. *Please, God, let them have mercy.* If they didn't, she'd make it all up anyway and say she was unconscious when she was injected. Besides, she barely remembered her own name when she awaked.

"What is it, doctor?" Did she really want to know?

"You're three months pregnant," he breathed, stumbling over the words as quickly he could. "I suggest that you stay here for a few more days so that we can get you started on the proper prenatal medications to clear your system of anything harmful and so that you can get yourself on your feet to take care of yourself for the sake of your child."

Sweet Jesus....

"I kept you when I could have given you up as I did with all the others! Everybody said I should have but, no, I wanted to do right by you. You didn't turn out to be worth the trouble. Biggs family pride at its best. I can't believe you've been running around like a tramp!"

Lela waved her hand to dismiss something Jasmine didn't see but kept talking. She first got wind of her daughter's sexual exploits in bits and pieces from eavesdropping. Initially, Lela was proud that her daughter was just as irresistible as she used to be and considered it, taboo as it may seem, a compliment. Soon, though, there were reports coming in from school concerning Jasmine entertaining boys in the bathroom and fighting other girls. One thing Lela wouldn't allow was her daughter being loose in public. The back seat of some boy's car was one thing but the bathroom... that was just despicable, and fighting was entirely out of the question.

When Lela finished reprimanding her daughter, Jasmine walked teary-eyed, back to her room. To make matters worse, that night her stepfather made an advance on her for the first time.

"Pregnant?"

"Yes, ma'am. Three months pregnant."

"With a baby?"

Jasmine couldn't believe what she was hearing. The doctor looked at her, frustrated with how dense she was being. The frustration registered in his voice.

"I promise you that the good people employed at this hospital can administer and read a pregnancy test, Miss Jefferson. You're one hundred percent pregnant and three months along. It's no wonder that you're oblivious to that fact, high as you were in this hospital three nights ago."

She knew that she was in trouble and was in over her head, but she didn't necessarily appreciate being chastised by anyone, even if the doctor was old enough to be her grandfather. She looked at him through squinted eyes and finally said, "There's no need to take that tone, sir."

He blanched slightly. He knew better. "I apologize, ma'am, but I do find it rather difficult that you could ignore three months without a menstrual cycle."

Jasmine had mastered ignoring what went on with her body a long time ago.

George Jefferson was the epitome of the angry, embittered serviceman; he had spent too much time in war and not enough time with humanity. His father was a general, and his grandfather was a sergeant. They reared him to believe that everything was a conquest and that especially women were placed on earth to be trapped, tamed, and trained. It made sense that he would chase after Lela Biggs-Templeton – it would be an attempt to subdue her wicked and sinful ways. If ever there was a woman worth trapping, it was Lela. All men praised her throughout as the best trick ever turned, but she was also very pretty and rumored "to come from money." His competition slimmed when she became and stayed pregnant, and for George Jefferson, the less competition, the better.

Her daughter was young by the time George and Lela said their hasty "I do's," so he agreed to adopting Jasmine and giving her his last name. But young Jasmine was starting to take after her mother in a myriad of ways – in numerous physical ways. He had inappropriate thoughts about her when he was alone and began comparing the aging Lela with the young and blossoming Jasmine. He knew that Jasmine's sexual activities were like her mother's as she was under boys too soon for the wrong reasons; he thought that if she got under a man, she'd be reassured that a boy wasn't worth her time. This skewed rationale was solid enough reason for him to abuse his stepdaughter for years. He only stopped after Lela found out and killed him, subsequently turning the gun on herself.

"So, you'll take care of me for a little bit longer at the hospital? I don't think I can afford that."

"Yes, we will. Your next of kin has already been contacted, and they have agreed to pay. A Miss Samantha Biggs?" he asked, reading the chart.

Holy shit. How did she become my next of kin? That bitch terrifies me.

Some of her trepidation must have reached her face because the doctor looked at her. "Miss Jefferson, is everything all right?"

170

No, I don't want to see that scary ass woman.

"Yes, sir, I just haven't seen my cousins in a long time." At least that wasn't a lie. "Did they say anything about Sarah Biggs?" *I'd prefer it if Sarah came down here.*

"Well, the names were on file from your mother's... incident a while back, I believe. That's where the police traced all of your information. Apparently, they only got in touch with Samantha."

"Oh, right." She wasn't listening to him anymore. *Damn.*

Samantha and Sarah Biggs came to visit their cousin Lela Biggs-Templeton Jefferson one morning in the unseasonably warm August heat. The shock was evident on Lela's face. You could never hide from Biggs' family genetics – the signs were undeniable. They shared the same features, the same eyes and hair. People often thought that they were inbred but later learned that there was a strategy to marrying a specific type of woman or man into the family, one with weak or plain genes. There were only a few members left of the Biggs' family, and Lela only wondered how these women at her door managed to find her.

"Are you Lela Biggs-Templeton?"

"Yes, yes I am. I mean I was...." The air almost escaped her entirely. She wanted to collapse and would have if Jasmine hadn't rounded the corner at that moment, bringing her back to earth.

"Mommy, who is that at the do…?" She stopped dead in her tracks. Before her were two women who looked as if they could have been her mother's sisters. The only difference was that there was so much anger and disgust etched in their faces. One had what looked to Jasmine to be a dead raccoon wrapped around her neck – *it is the middle of August; is she cold* – and the other one slanted her eyes at Jasmine and scowled. The women at the door looked down at Jasmine, and she gasped in surprise. These women were clearly incredibly scary.

"We're your cousins, honey," Samantha said, exasperated. "Would you like to invite us in, or are you going to let us stand forever in this heat?"

"Oh, yes, of course." Lela had no idea what to make of these powerful women at her doorstep. She turned around and did a hasty cleaning, tossing things off the couch and onto the floor. Jasmine sprang into action as well, hoping that picking up things would give her the opportunity to leave the room. She was genuinely frightened.

"Lela, I'm thirsty. Send that little one to get me something to drink," Sarah said, offering Jasmine a half smile. Jasmine wanted to whimper.

Jasmine happily obliged without her mother saying anything. Lela was astonished, frustrated, and hurt all at once. She didn't appreciate being

172

commanded by her younger cousins, but she couldn't do anything more than to obey. These twins were not to be trifled with. They still hadn't introduced themselves, either.

"We're Sarah and Samantha Biggs," Samantha said dryly, looking at a large stain on the floor and gnawing mindlessly on a fingernail on her right hand. They were dressed in fancy dresses, the kind of attire you would wear to a party in New Orleans. They were too flashy to be in her dingy living room. *What on earth do they want?*

"Hello, Sarah and Samantha."

"My sister is just a bit tired. We've had a trying day," Sarah explained. She was gnawing on the same finger as her sister but on her left hand and had the courtesy to look Lela in the face. It was quite the sight. They were terrifyingly identical.

"So, what brings you to Louisiana?"

"How would you know we even left?" Samantha snapped. Sarah patted her sister's knee and whispered something about being calm.

"I was really just asking," Lela stammered. The cruelty in Samantha's voice was palpable, and Lela was relieved when Jasmine returned from the kitchen with the good sense to bring lemonade for everyone in the room on the one good tray.

"Well, we have been in Chicago for a while. Those Italian boys like taking care of us," Sarah said, batting her lashes and giggling as though the very same 'boys' were walking into the room. It occurred to Lela that Sarah might be high.

"I see," said Lela. "You all have on some lovely dresses."

"Why, thank you Lela," Samantha said coolly, "I'm glad you think so."

Lela ignored Samantha, seeing that Sarah was the one worth talking to, even if she was high. She knew that if there were any battles to be won, she'd want Sarah on her side, at minimum. "So, Sarah, how may I help you two?"

"Straight to the point, like a true Biggs," Sarah smiled and giggled. "Me and Samantha just wanted to come and see you. We like to establish family relations like Momma and Daddy said we should. We wanted to send our brother down here, but we will do that later. We thought we'd see you first. There are only a handful of us pure Biggses left, after all," and she sighed heavily, staring pointedly at Jasmine when she said pure.

"This is very true," Lela agreed, still not clearly seeing where the conversation was going. "Well, I'm glad to oblige if you'd like to play catch up," she started.

When Sarah and Samantha leaned in, keen to learn more, Lela knew that she'd hit her mark. The three of them spoke easily for hours about all of the Biggs' family, the twin's father, Everson, and Lela's father, Nelson, who passed before Everson was born. Lela never talked about her father, Everson's lost sister's husband. It made her sad to think about him and her and the way that they'd been cast from the family for reasons unknown.

Jasmine gleaned much of her family history from that conversation since she'd never asked her mother about it before. After the twins left, her mother gave her even more information. When she finally met her cousin Zebedee Biggs, she recognized him immediately but knew that it wouldn't be worth it to talk to him. She was mainly afraid that he'd be as frightening as his older sisters, and she hated him instantly for dating a Woods sister.

"Well, Miss Jefferson, I will step out and see if your family has arrived. Also, an officer will be by to take your statement. You weren't coherent enough when you first arrived here."

"Thank you, doctor," she said quietly

She breathed deeply and involuntarily clutched her belly. *You're three months pregnant, Jasmine. There's a baby squirming around somewhere in there, and you might have killed it by sniffing coke. You're doing a great job, genius.*

She was halted mid-deprecation. Somehow, tears were forming in her eyes and spilling down her cheeks – twenty-six years of hurt and confusion and a pain that dug into her heart. She had never cried, even when her stepfather was raping her. She dug holes for everything, saving the pain for some other time and allowing herself to believe that she was only living life. Now, she was going to be a mother and she had to be strong. She knew that, if anything, she had to be good to herself so that she could be good to this child.

"Good God, are you crying?"

Jasmine was startled from her deep thoughts, and she looked up. *Wow.* Samantha Biggs was greatly diminished from the time that Jasmine first met her as a child. Her overbearing frame had withdrawn to make way for a whimpering cat woman. The same coldness lurked behind her eyes, and she was no beauty. Her skin was wrinkled and sagged. She smelled like cigarettes, and her clothes were too big for her. Still, Jasmine knew that there was probably more money in that handbag dangling precariously from her cousin's wrist than she'd ever had for herself.

"Cousin Samantha?"

"Yeah, kid. Let's skip the obvious." There it was. *Straight to the point, like a true Biggs.*

"How are you? Where is Sarah?"

Samantha stopped and looked momentarily alarmed. Then, she took a deep breath and hurriedly said, "She died from that same stuff they said you've been sniffing. I'm fine. Don't ask."

Jasmine knew that this was not a request, so she changed the pace, determined to stand her ground.

"Thank you for taking care of everything at the hospital."

"Honestly, kid, I don't exactly have a choice. This is what the Biggs' family does for one another, no matter how fucked up the last few of us are. It's not out of caring; it's out of obligation. Don't get all mushy about it." She was chewing on her finger.

"I didn't think I was pure enough to be counted as a Biggs," Jasmine spat out.

"My, so she does have a backbone," Samantha cackled. "Kitty's got claws, huh?"

Jasmine was silent.

"Kitty's also got a baby, hasn't she," and Samantha reached out a withered hand to touch Jasmine's belly but recoiled when Jasmine swatted at her.

"Don't act like a baby when you're about to have one," Samantha admonished. "You're in no position to act like that with me."

"Fine." Jasmine wasn't entirely convinced that she wanted her nearest relation around. *Maybe Samantha should have died.* Wishful thinking never did Jasmine any good.

"Well, anyway, I came down here to give you this. If you use it right, it will settle you for a lifetime. Or, at least, until you find a damn job." Samantha tossed the handbag to Jasmine who struggled to catch it. She was still bruised all over and very sore. She hadn't yet so much as sat up from the bed.

On opening the bag, Jasmine's jaw dropped. There was easily fifty thousand dollars crammed into the bag and what looked like a satchel of diamonds. *Are those diamonds?*

"Yes, they're diamonds. They're some from the family vault. Forgive me for keeping the best for myself," she gloated, holding up one wrinkled middle finger to reveal a gigantic stone.

"I didn't even know that diamonds came that big," Jasmine said stupidly.

"I didn't know you knew what diamonds were," Samantha quipped.

Jasmine gathered what was left of her confidence.

"If you didn't want to see me then, you shouldn't have come. Nobody asked you to be here, so don't get snippy with me you wicked old witch. I don't have the energy to get up and whip you, but if I did, your ass would be grass, understand?" Every bit of Louisiana was hanging from her words. She watched her cousin's face go from firm to flat in a matter of moments, her jaw dropping lower and lower with every word.

"Kitty's got claws and what's more is Kitty's moving into the Biggs' family house in Shreveport. You and Kitty are going to stay there, and you'll say nothing to the contrary."

"Now, you just wait one minute, young lady."

"No, ma'am, you wait. I hope you don't think I forgot that you treated my momma and me like the scum of the earth when you met us. And to think, I found out that you and Sarah were the biggest whores in the city of Chicago. Well, now it's time for you to pay up. I hope you didn't think this little bit of hush money was going to handle anything. Hell, I don't even know if these are real diamonds. So, you, old wench, are going to be stuck with me and your baby cousin in here," she patted her belly, satisfied, "and you're going to get a little bit of docility and some domesticity about you, and you're going to learn what family loyalty really looks like."

The old woman staggered back into a chair that was placed against the wall. Jasmine was glad that the door was closed.

"How old are you, Samantha?"

Since she was dumbstruck, Samantha answered without an attitude. "I'm sixty-seven years old."

"Well, you're going to stop smoking so you can reach sixty-eight years old, and you're going to be the family that I never had for this child."

Samantha felt as though she'd been slapped. She hadn't expected this behavior from someone more than forty years her junior. She anticipated dropping the money off and leaving. Now, she had sobering thoughts of her sister and the way that the two of them shriveled up together, never having a

179

child and never bothering to stay true to their family values even if some of them were unspeakable. She didn't know if she was prepared for it. What her cousin said was true – she was nothing more than a bitter old hag. She should at least give this a shot. She could always leave.

"So, what, am I going to be? The kid's grandma, since your mother blew her head off?"

"Yes, exactly and you should watch your fucking mouth about my mother," Jasmine said, a thin line taking the space where her mouth should have been. Then, she softened and smirked eventually giving way to laughter. Samantha found herself laughing, too.

"Well," Samantha sighed, standing slowly and making her way over to the bed, "you must be a Biggs. That was surely straight to the point." She extended her hand.

"My thoughts exactly," Jasmine said. They shook, the old wrinkled hand clasping the bruised and broken one, making their final amends across family lines.

Chapter 24

The French Quarter was bustling with activity, filled to the brim with tourists and natives alike. The family couldn't contain their excitement. The Woods sisters, family, and friends occupied the better part of the streets as they paraded the children around the Quarter, explaining where they were and the history of the area. Felicity warned that everyone should enjoy Louisiana while they could. Soon, they'd all be in South Carolina enjoying Charleston and the Atlantic Ocean – Anthony and Felicity, Mahogany, Maxine and Carl, Jones, Melody, and Ebony with all five of her children – enjoying the sun, the water, and the good times together. But for right now, everyone wanted a piece of Louisiana.

Unsurprisingly, Ebony managed to plan three perfect weddings in one weekend and created a feeling of love in the air of New Orleans. Anthony and Felicity didn't ask for much; Felicity was happy her family was together, and Anthony was happy to be with Felicity. To even out the numbers for his guests, he invited Jones, his fiancée Melody, and his estranged brothers. Jones, especially, was surprised to see together the James boys.

"The more white people, the more likely we are to be on time," he chuckled.

"Watch your mouth, Jones," Anthony said through slanted eyes.

"We have to invite them, Anthony. Here, let me straighten your tie."

They stepped out from the repast that was going on in the church basement. Felicity was wearing a black dress and a hat with a black veil, which covered her eyes. Mahogany and Felicity were wearing the same hat, and even Ebony arrived similarly dressed. Anthony thought about how close they were, how they dressed alike even after years of being far apart. He didn't have that type of relationship with his brothers. There was always a very strict distinction; he was the momma's boy and the baby while his brothers were cast in their father's image. Anthony hadn't spoken to them in years, and their only communications were stereotyped Christmas cards complete with a picture of their growing families – even those were mailed to his office and not to his apartment. Mitchell had three children and was married twice; Barry had four children but hadn't been married. *Or was it the other way around?* Would bringing them to his wedding be a good idea? He let out a small groan.

"Anthony, they need to come. My family's here and if I'm going to be Mrs. James, I should at least know what my brothers-in-law look like."

182

She had a point, but there were other things on his mind. What would his brothers think of his bride and her family? What would they think of him? Did it even matter? He shuddered.

"Let me think about it, baby. I need time to think."

She pouted at him, but she eventually nodded and stopped fidgeting with his tie. He grabbed her hand and kissed it lightly, and they walked back into the repast.

Anthony didn't bother to tell Felicity that they would be flying to the Western coast of Africa after they left Charleston or that, following that adventure, they'd be off to tour Europe. Jones and Melody would be waiting for them in France since that was the only place Melody really wanted to visit. He was proud that his friend made amends with Melody even if their vows were hasty. Jones reasoned that he'd rather be with someone that drove him crazy; Anthony allowed it because that was the way Jones did things. To Jones, his was the type of logic that would last a lifetime and didn't need questioning, so Anthony settled. While they walked through Charleston's streets together, watching the expert basket weavers and picking up small, carved goods here and there, Anthony considered hinting to his wife that she would need something more appropriate for the climes they'd be entering soon. He didn't want to ruin the surprise, but she would need something a bit more than Converse if they were going to Cote d'Ivore. Afterward, they were off to Morocco and, shortly after, Spain.

"This is Barry." His brother's voice was even deeper than he remembered. After a great deal of confusing conversation between Anthony and who he thought was his sister-in-law, Anthony finally got his brother on the phone.

"Hey, Barry. It's um.... It's Anthony."

"Anthony who?"

"Um, Barry, it's me. It's the Ant. Your baby brother, Anthony the Ant."

After a pause, wild laughter broke out in his ear.

"Baby brother, where have you been hiding? And why is this the first time you're calling? I'm going to have to write this down. It's a new holiday."

The response was much warmer and overwhelming than anticipated, but Anthony still felt guilty. Had he been hiding from his brothers? *Surely we all just went our separate ways. I wasn't hiding from anyone; I'm a grown man.* He decided that his brother was joking and that it would be better to make light of the situation.

"No, Barry, I haven't been hiding. Who answered the phone?" The woman who answered seemed to be under the impression that Barry's only brother

184

was Mitchell. It was an easy mistake to make – Barry and Mitchell had the same build, and they both owned consulting firms. Barry's offices were in New Jersey, and Mitchell stationed his operation in upstate New York. They were alike in every way except the color of their eyes and hair. Mitchell allowed his grays to show through his dark brown hair, but Barry chopped his hair off entirely at the first sign of age, preferring a "timeless image." Anthony wouldn't have fit into their perfect picture.

"That was Christine. She's my new girlfriend. She loves the kids. There are too many of them for me to count or take care of. She looked awfully confused when she handed me the phone."

"Yeah, I don't think she knew you and Mitch had another brother."

"Well, I can only wonder why."

Anthony frowned. Barry had lived in New Jersey for over twenty years and still held on to his deep southern accent. He sounded like their father.

"Look, Barry, I know that I should have called and kept in touch, but I just never fit in with you and Mitch. You know that."

"Ant, you always fit in. You're our brother. Genetically, you fit in."

Anthony felt smaller and smaller. He didn't like being reprimanded; however, he couldn't ignore the truth. Every year, his brothers sent him holiday cards, and they would reach out with birthday cards on the 'big' years like his twenty-first birthday and his twenty-fifth. He never called back or reached out at all.

The truth was that he avoided his brothers because they were everything his father wanted, and he didn't see any of himself in them. Now, more than ever, he wanted his family to be with him, but years of self-alienation and efforts to avoid them at all costs made them feel unwelcome in his life. *Too much that needs fixing...*

"Look, Barry, I'm sorry that I didn't reach out and keep you and Mitch involved in my life. It was wrong of me, and I shouldn't have done that to you. You're my brothers, and even though we don't like the same things, we are in the same family, and I love you. I really do."

"Aw, nobody told you to get all mushy on me, Ant," mocked Barry. He was teasing him, but you could hear small hints of appreciation in his voice. "So, you finally called. I'm guessing you need something. What happened? Did all the airplanes you built fall out of the sky?" Anthony's ear rang once more with his brother's outrageous laughter.

"Actually, no, I'm getting married."

Barry's laughter abruptly stopped and gave way to a fit of chokes and coughs. As he struggled to maintain his composure, Anthony smiled. Barry was always the brother that preferred to be single but wanted a house full of children. He changed

186

girlfriends in high school every two weeks, and in college, he didn't even have one. The college years were dedicated to studying and getting out into the big leagues; girls had never fit into that picture. He idly wondered how long he'd been dating Christine.

Anthony was just starting middle school when Barry went off to Rutgers. Right behind him, two years later, Mitchell went to Columbia, and the rest was history. Anthony was the only one that stayed in state for the sake of being close to his mother. She was his only family next to Jones and Mrs. Brown. He had no reason to leave Mississippi until his business progressed. When his mother died, Anthony sat in the back of the church and avoided his brothers. He was heart-broken and sorry that she wouldn't see his grandchildren but happy that they wouldn't be with Charlotte. *Speaking of which...*

"Good God, Anthony, you're not marrying that she-devil Charlotte are you?"

Now it was his turn to laugh. "No, Barry. My fiancée's name is Felicity. She's from Louisiana. That's actually where I am now. I know it is short notice, but do you think you could make it?"

"He doesn't want his brothers to come? Why? Is he ashamed of you?"

"See, there you go. Of course, I'm the only person he could possibly be ashamed of, right? There couldn't be any other reason why he wouldn't want

187

his brothers to come except keeping them away from me? What about trying to keep them away from you and your big mouth? Maybe that's why he's hiding them."

Walking in on the middle of a Woods sisters' argument was never safe. *They need caution lights or something.* Felicity and Mahogany were battling it out while Ebony sat in the chair feeding Teresa and Dennis and pretending not to be involved. Both of the children's eyes were wide with amazement. *I'm enjoying the battle of wills, too, kids.*

"All I'm saying is he needs to get over it. I don't know what he's trying to hide or whom, but it's not appropriate for him to marry you and not have any family here."

"What about his parents?" Ebony chimed in. The three of them were still unaware that Anthony was standing in the doorway. He thought it would be a good time to intervene.

"They passed a long time ago." His voice made Ebony and Mahogany jump, but Felicity simply hung her head.

"See, now he heard you. Apologize, Mahogany."

"Who are you giving orders to? I'm nine years older than you!"

"She doesn't really need to apologize if he didn't hear anything."

"Whose side are you on?"

"She doesn't need to pick sides."

Oh, this will never end. "Enough!"

All three women jumped this time. Anthony was the center of attention now, standing in Carl's dining room with one hand on his hip and one hand on his head. He was frustrated after making phone calls to his brothers. Barry only agreed to come if they split the airfare down the middle or if Anthony could get them a discount on the tickets. Mitch didn't pick up on the first ring but called back while Anthony was leaving a message. Mitch was less forgiving than Barry.

"I've called my brothers and they're coming. No, my not inviting them sooner has nothing to do with any of you. It's just a very last minute arrangement if all of this is going to be happening in two weeks. I was not trying to offend any of you. This whole month has just been very stressful for me, and I would like to end it on a positive note."

Felicity began studying something with her foot on the floor, and Ebony pretended to be too busy again, feeding her children. Only Mahogany glared at Anthony.

"Well, fine. At least you're not a spineless joke like Jonathan or that partner of yours who is ready to marry every girl that gets in bed with him."

Felicity and Ebony gasped. "Mahogany!"

Jones went to the IEEE/AIAA conference alone, but he called Anthony in the middle of the week to

189

announce his own engagement to Melody. It was a shock for which Anthony wasn't prepared.

"I left you for all of five days, and you mean to tell me that you are trying to tie the knot all of a sudden?"

"Look, Ant, it's a long story, but it's your and Felicity's fault. I want some marital bliss, too. Besides, Melody is game for it."

"Which means you bought her a huge ring."

"Do you have to ruin everything with technicalities?"

Anthony chuckled.

"Think we can squeeze another wedding into your weekend?"

The day of the wedding was chaotic. Felicity wouldn't talk to him, and his brothers were too busy drunkenly complaining about not being men of honor to notice that they were spilling champagne on his cummerbund. *I shouldn't have let them near the bar.*

"All I'm saying is we're your brothers, and you are letting that goofball Jones do our job?" Mitch was slurring his words and stumbling over imaginary objects. Before the contents of his drink could spill on and damage the rest of Anthony's suit, he yanked it all from the bed and glared at the less inebriated Barry who quickly sat Mitch down and took away his glass.

190

"That's enough, little brother," Barry grinned. "I think Ant has heard enough."

"Anthony the Ant! Do you remember when we used to call you that?" Mitch was doubled over with laughter.

"Barry, fix him." Anthony fumed, marching into the bathroom and slamming the door behind him. He was emotional; his nerves had him shaking, and he couldn't seem to get his bowtie tied correctly. He was just about to give up when a soft knock on the door tore him away from his frustrations.

"What is it, Barry?"

"This isn't Barry."

Anthony pulled open the door. *She cleans up nicely.*

Mahogany was standing in the doorway with a new cummerbund in hand and a smirk on her face. "Mind if I make you pretty, brother-in-law?"

Anthony grimaced. He still wasn't pleased with Mahogany. She was as bad as Jones had been when Felicity stepped into the picture; she made it a point to antagonize Anthony about dating her baby sister when it was no longer pertinent and told him that, had her father been alive, he wouldn't have approved of their union, let alone their dating. Anthony grinned and got through it while Felicity bared her teeth and cussed at her sister every time she had the chance. *At least she is willing to fight for you.*

191

"If you insist on dressing me like a toddler, I will allow it only under the condition that you don't go about telling people that you did so because I'm somehow incapable."

"Or, perhaps I will tell them that I dressed you because your brother is so drunk that he ruined your outfit with his inability to hold light liquor." She smiled. She had a pretty smile. She just didn't like him.

"Fine," he pouted, stepping aside so that she could get into the bathroom.

She knows what she's doing, at least. Mahogany replaced Anthony's soiled cummerbund with the newly laundered one and knotted his bowtie perfectly. She brought his jacket together and fixed his pants, but she stopped when she got to his hair.

"My daddy didn't have hair like that so um.... You're on your own."

Anthony frowned at her. *We were just starting to get along. Why would you bring that up?*

"So, you learned how to do all this with your father?"

Mahogany nodded, sullenly. "Yes. After Momma died, there was nobody else to do it for him." She was very quiet, and her attitude shift changed the atmosphere in the bathroom; she no longer looked thirty-five. "Felicity will be looking for me," she said suddenly, jumping into action and springing for the door.

"Wait!"

Anthony reached out and grabbed her shoulder, but he wasn't entirely sure what he wanted to say.

"I know that you don't particularly care for me," – *yes, that's a good place to start* – "and I know that you don't think that I will do a good job of taking care of your sister the way you and your father took care of her."

Mahogany turned around, her eyes wide, but her facial expression was otherwise unreadable.

"I just want you to know that I have no intention of replacing anyone. I am just here to be everything else for Felicity. She's always going to need you and Ebony to be her sisters, and she will always look to the past and think of her father when she needs strength. But I'm here to be everything else. I'm here to hold her and tell her I love her and give her everything she wants. It's my job to spoil her and take care of her when you're not around. If you don't think I'm up to the job, that's fine. However, I hope you understand that I didn't come down here to seek your approval. I'm here to marry the woman I love."

A small tear threatened to escape from Mahogany's right eye, but she shook her head and nodded.

"Okay, I get it, white boy. You're here for good."

193

She patted his hand and he released her. She got to the door and opened it slightly, but then she turned back around.

"But if you hurt my sister, I'm fucking you up."

With that, she stomped out and slammed the door.

"I love it here. It's so beautiful."

The Moroccan sun was good to Felicity's skin. Anthony, however, suffered a bit. Somewhere along the line, he lost his sunscreen, and he was beginning to burn. His only relief was the breeze that came through and the small breeze being generated by Felicity's waving hand in front of his face. *I know I'm the color of an apple right now.*

"Honey, let's go back to the hotel. We need to get you some sunscreen or something. I don't want you to burn."

"No, I am fine, Miss Lady. I will be okay. No need to cut your fun short."

She pouted to object but didn't say anything. He didn't realize why until they got back to the small street where their hotel was located and she pulled him in by force. "I dare you to argue with me," she said, threatening to kiss his burned nose.

"No, no need to argue," he said, pulling away quickly. *I can't believe she led me right back here without my even noticing.* Felicity Woods just had that effect on people.

194

When they got to the airport in South Carolina, Felicity slowly put the pieces together. They boarded a flight to LaGuardia, which Anthony tried to disguise as part of a one-stop flight back to Houston. When they headed toward the international gates, however, he couldn't disguise it any longer. Felicity swung around, her eyes blazing and dropping her bag in amazement.

"Where are we going? You have to tell me right now! What did you do?"

Her voice was getting louder and louder, and she was beaming. People began to take notice.

"Mrs. James, I'd appreciate it if you kept it down," he whispered, pulling her in and taming her flailing arms. He kissed her forehead, and she immediately calmed down.

"Okay, I'm calm. Now, tell me where you're taking me."

"Hola, Senora. ¿Como fue la playa? ¿Compraste nuevos zapatos?"

"No, no. Son los mismos. La playa, ¿que puedo decir? El mar es maravillosa. ¿y la gente? Nadie es mas agradable de lo que son."

She is perfect. I will never have another love like this. Felicity James is my one and only. They were in Cadiz and Felicity was showing off. He felt a little bit out of place as she carried on with the woman that

195

ran the small motel, but he didn't mind watching her carry on in a language he barely understood. When she first told him she spoke Spanish and Italian, he dedicated himself to learning the very minimum of both languages so that he could at least greet people and tell them that he was enjoying the weather. Beyond that, Felicity took over.

"Miss Lady, I'm going upstairs. I'm a little tired." He hoped that would be enough of a hint that it was time to go.

"Oh, okay, honey. I'm coming. Hasta luego, Pilar."

Pilar smiled and offered a small wave before she attended to her other guests. Their room was small, but they didn't need much space; there would be plenty of room in their suite at Hotel Lutetia. The next day they would be off to Paris to meet with Melody and Jones. That night they stayed awake laughing about Anthony's sunburn incidents in both Cote d'Ivore and Morocco and Felicity's unfortunate incident with a cross-dressing man on the plane.

"This is an amazing honeymoon, Anthony," she purred, wrapping tightly around him and resting her head on his chest.

"Beats cow-tipping, huh?"

They both laughed and continued to reminisce until they both fell asleep.

UNFINISHED PROJECTS

After further discussing it with his senselessly drunk brothers, Anthony agreed to allow them to stand behind him as groomsmen during the ceremony. He asked Melody to stand with Felicity's sisters, and it was only after several objections and the necessary compliments on the dress she was wearing that didn't match Ebony or Mahogany's that she agreed. *Now, it's even and no one else should be complaining.*

Before he could make his way downstairs into the small ballroom to take his place before the minister, Ebony came running toward him. *What now? What could possibly be wrong, now?*

"It's Felicity. She needs to talk to you right now!"

Without hesitation, Anthony ran to Mahogany's room where all the women were getting ready, and he knocked frantically.

"Felicity, honey, what's wrong?"

"Don't break the door down, man. Are you crazy?" Mahogany hollered from inside.

Ebony slipped passed him and unlocked the door. "It's just Ebony. I'm coming in."

She slammed the door behind her. Anthony waved his hands in the air, utterly flabbergasted. *Honestly.* There was shuffling and muttering, and Anthony couldn't distinguish a word. He heard sobbing and assumed that Felicity was crying. There were only fifteen minutes left before they were to be blissfully wed. Was she having second thoughts?

"Anthony?"

"Yes, baby, I'm here. What's wrong?" His heart was palpitating as his fears were confirmed by the sadness and hesitation in her voice. "What's going on, baby?"

She sniffed then, "I just wanted to say that I'm really scared. I mean I love you, but I am really scared."

Oh no. His heart plunged.

"I'm scared, too. But, I will tell you a secret."

His fear of rejection decreased. *She still loves you, Ant. Just make her smile and tell her you're not going anywhere so we can get this show on the road.*

"What's that?"

"Everybody is scared on her wedding day. It's all the amazing things that happen after the wedding that make it okay. We're going to be okay!" By saying it aloud, he quelled his own fears, which had gone unacknowledged until that very moment.

"How do you know, though? I mean, Jones doesn't like me, and your brothers don't know me. What if everything falls apart?"

"If it falls apart, then we are just going to have to put it back together, aren't we?" There were now ten minutes on the clock. *Come on, baby. Don't give up on me now.*

"Will you pray with me?"

What?

"I just want you to pray with me, and if you do, I know it will be okay."

The last time Anthony prayed, he was six. His mother took him to service every Sunday as a devout Catholic until he was seven, and he decided that he would much rather celebrate God at home by way of Christmas and Sunday radio specials. The only other woman he ever heard pray was Mrs. Brown, and her prayers were very different from his mother's. Felicity never asked him to pray before. He didn't even think that she was particularly religious. *Okay, if it's prayer my lady wants, then it's prayer my lady gets.*

"Open the door and give me your hand, Felicity."

There was more shuffling, and he heard her blow her nose. *I hope I don't get that hand.* She opened the door and stuck out her small left hand.

"It's clean, I promise." She was giggling a little. He was going to win this battle with her fear.

"Okay, you ready?"

He took her hand and smiled down at the Mikimoto ring that he presented her almost a month ago. He was happy she was still wearing it because it was another sign that she wasn't going anywhere. "Okay, bow your head and close your eyes."

He couldn't see her but assumed that she had and tried to remember a prayer. All that came to mind was all that he said, a combination of Mrs. Brown and his mother.

"Lord, we come to you today in the name of your son Jesus the Christ that you might bless the matrimony between this man and this woman on this the twelfth day in the month of July among their family and friends. May you smite our enemies and oppressors and have the bartender think it not robbery to give me some liquid courage. We ask that the hearts of Anthony Bruce James and Felicity Irene Woods be united and on one accord moving forward from this day on and that there be good food." He pried open one eye as Felicity squeezed his hand and giggled uncontrollably.

"Father, forgive my foolish husband. Say 'amen!' Anthony."

"In Jesus's name we pray, amen!"

"Amen."

"I wish I could see your face right now."

"Oh, I promise you don't," she laughed again, sniffling. At least he knew she was smiling. She pulled her hand away. "Besides," she continued, "it's bad luck to see me in my dress."

"I don't think it's good to talk about luck after you pray, Miss lady."

"Good bye, Mr. James," she giggled.

"I will see you downstairs, Mrs. James." Even though it wasn't official yet, he liked the sound of it.

There was only one minute to show time; he was going to have to make a run for it.

"Anthony, do you take Felicity Irene Woods for your lawful wedded wife, to live in the holy estate of matrimony? Will you love, honor, comfort, and cherish her from this day forward, forsaking all others, keeping only unto her for as long as you both shall live?"

"I do." *Come on, man.*

He was ready to pounce on Felicity. He was ready for this. She was everything he could have ever asked for or wanted. Anything that he sought in another woman, she had already. All he had to do was go to Jeffries' office to find her, and she would have been waiting for him there. He would have waited forever for her.

"Felicity, do you take Anthony Bruce James for your lawful wedded husband, to live in the holy estate of matrimony? Will you love, honor, comfort, and cherish him from this day forward, forsaking all others, keeping only unto him for as long as you both shall live?"

Mahogany sniffled and Ebony patted her on the back. He could sense Mitch and Barry teetering in the background. *Please don't let them fall over.*

"I do."

Okay, the rings are both on and so am I. Once they kissed, it would be permanent. He would live his dream with his dream girl. This was neither a bad summer vacation nor a bad way to live.

"By the power vested in me, I now pronounce you husband and wife. You may kiss the bride." *Finally.*

The kiss was very brief, but it was only because Felicity, who was beautifully gowned in all lace with the second set of pearls he gave her dangling from her ears and covering her neck, pulled away.

"I hope you won't need any liquid courage tonight." There was a flicker in her eyes. *Gamine.*

"No, woman, now give me my kiss."

Chapter 25

"Okay, Jones. What is going on? We've been all over the city of Houston today. You won't tell me why you have been dragging me through the streets or why it is that I've been allowed to stay over every night since last Friday when you took me out." Melody was chasing him through the apartment from his bedroom until he finally paused at the refrigerator in the kitchen.

"Yes. It's Wednesday, now. Are you going to stay over again?" He stooped down and pulled out the orange juice and poured himself a glass.

"Well... I...." She started stuttering. "Only if you tell me what's going on!" She stomped her foot down, her heel making a small crack on the tiles in his kitchen.

"Lower your voice, Melody and don't stomp. You're going to scare the people downstairs." He grinned sadistically.

He was enjoying torturing her. She always asked too many questions, but he loved it when she talked incessantly. It was the best way to wake up, the best way to go to sleep, and the best way to spend the day. She would send essays in emails and text messages in short story format, and he would respond with one word or one sentence just so that she could rant again. It was miraculous that she was still gainfully employed since she clearly couldn't be paying attention if she was writing him all day. Even if she was behind a desk and no one knew what she was doing, she couldn't be very productive. *I don't want her to work anymore. She doesn't have to. Not with this new deal between Anthony and me. Melody Jones doesn't sound half bad.* He started to grin.

"Aloysius Isaiah Jones the Third, are you laughing at me?" She had a hand on her hip.

He struggled to swallow his juice and hastily put the glass down so that he wouldn't drop it. "Woman, did you just say my full name?"

She was giggling now. How could he even pretend to be angry at that smile and that face? There was no logical reason to be annoyed, really. She had more power over him than he cared to admit, but she did everything in her power to keep him happy. It was the reason he didn't care whether or not she would yell at him one day and come back the next ready to apologize and make up for it. He still regretted telling her his whole name, though.

"Okay, you want to know what's going on?" Jones stood up and walked over to her. Melody backed up, scared that she might have started something she couldn't finish.

"Yes," she whimpered. She bit down on her thumb and glanced nervously at him. He was standing directly in front of her just before he dropped to one knee. Melody's jaw dropped; it was the second time in less than a week that he'd seen her speechless.

"This is what's going on."

They were dining at Del Frisco's. Melody was wary. She clearly didn't trust the suddenly generous treatment she was receiving from Jones. This was the one restaurant she always begged him to take her to, and he would never do it. Now, he'd made reservations, and there was wine available on the table. He decided to overlook her nervousness and insisted on ordering for her so that the waitress would be gone and he could speak his piece. She didn't object. *This is it.* He rubbed his hands together and looked at her. He remembered all the reasons why he called her and what he really wanted to say, but he only uttered one thing.

"I want you to be my girlfriend, and I refuse to take no for an answer."

Melody's jaw might as well have hit the table. Her mouth was wide open. *Is this really all that surprising? I've been an asshole to her. Now is not the time to keep these thoughts to myself.*

"Listen, I called you earlier to apologize because I am genuinely sorry. I treated you horribly for the past year. Honestly, you deserve one hundred times better than what I gave you, and I didn't give you much. I didn't give you anything. I'd like to change that."

205

Melody closed her mouth but continued to stare at him completely dumbstruck and remained surprisingly quiet. *I don't think she's ever been this quiet around me before. Keep it going, Jones. Say what you need to say.*

"I have lied to you before. Give me the chance to be honest with you. I want to tell you everything. I bet you don't even know my full name. I will tell it to you right now. I will tell you everything you want to know. You can come over and stay over. We can go to the movies. We can do anything you want to do. I just want you to understand that you're all I'm thinking about, that you're all I want, and that all the women in the world don't compare to you."

Melody blinked hard and put her hands on the table as if trying to steady herself. *What is she thinking? Please say something.*

"Did I screw up that badly?"

Before Jones could finish his thoughts, Melody started laughing. It was full-fledged, raucous laughter that was directed at Jones and not to be shared with him. He could hardly swallow. She was frustrating him. *Why won't she say anything?*

"Jones, you are something else." Her eyebrow was arched, and she was smirking.

Melody's gorgeous face and her long black hair gave her the illusion of being some sort of Arabian goddess. She was adopted, and her parents told her that she was of mixed heritage, but she preferred to check off the 'black' box on the census. It was her way of weeding out the prejudiced business owners before she went to work for them. She was proud of her identity, proud to be a poor girl from Chicago who paid her own way through college and made money like a real hustler. She was street smart and didn't take grief from anyone until she met Jones. Somehow, she had a soft spot in her heart for him, one that he always weaseled his way back into.

"You call me to take me to dinner, and now we're at dinner and you ask me to be your girl. You do realize the last time we spoke you were kicking me out of your apartment, right?" Her voice was like a taste of Chicago. Her eyebrow was still peaked, daring him to object.

"Melody, I'm just being honest with you." Jones was begging. This was new for everyone at the table.

"If you're going to be honest with me, then you need to tell me how you got to this magical place where you want to sprinkle fairy dust and wave a wand to make us better. Because up until just now, I thought you were trifling. Now, I know you're just psychotic." Sarcasm was dripping from every word.

She was cutting deep but she always had. *I thought Felicity was brutal. Damn. I'd take Felicity's eye roll to this any day.*

"Okay, you want me to tell you how I got here. It's going to be hard to do that without sounding cheesy but...."

"Sound cheesy. Honesty isn't always supposed to sound cool. It's not the most sought after human trait, but you offered it and I want it, so pay up."

Jones sat back in his seat and swallowed. It was a tall order, but he had offered it. What exactly did being honest entail? What all did she want to know of what he kept from her? Was she really that much better than he was?

"What do you want to know?"

She paused for a moment. "I want to see your driver's license."

"What?" *This is preposterous. That has nothing to do with us.*

"If I'm going to get to know you and we're going to be honest, I want to know your real name. I know for a fact that your mother wasn't so countrified that she named you Jones."

"How would you know that?" He was laughing, but he found himself pulling out his wallet, nevertheless. *She wants the license; then, she'll get the license.* To his surprise, she was also removing her license.

"Okay, switch." She was playful now and looked visibly relieved. She even took off her jacket. He liked her this way. He liked a number of things about her.

208

"Aloysius?"

"Hey, look. I can't even pronounce your middle name. Does this say Pal-o-mine?"

They were both laughing now.

"Wake up, Melody. It's time for breakfast."

He was standing over her in basketball shorts and a white tank top. She was just starting to open her eyes when he bent over and scooped her out of the bed. She kicked in protest, but he only squeezed her more tightly.

"Jones, put me down!"

Her hair was wild, and with all the shaking she was doing, it was only getting worse. She was hitting his chest playfully, but he knew that she was more likely to awake fully that way. He'd cooked for her because he wanted her up and eating. There was a big day ahead of them; Jones planned to take her to Galveston for the day. He wanted to take her to the beach and see all of the beautiful skin on her body. Most importantly, he wanted to show her off.

"Honestly, Jones, I could have walked," she groaned as he sat her in the chair at the dining room table. *I know that, silly.* He smiled at her and couldn't resist planting a kiss on her forehead. She smiled in defeat and dropped her shoulders. "So, I'm up. Where's my breakfast?"

Jones ran into the kitchen and retrieved two large plates. "Right here."

209

Piled high on each plate were scrambled eggs, bacon, toast, and grits. After putting his own plate down, he ran back into the kitchen and returned with two bowls full of fruit: blueberries, strawberries?" and pineapples. On his final trip, he came back with napkins and silverware and laid them out on the table like a trained busboy.

"Did you cook this?" She already forked two massive heaps of food into her mouth. He realized that he'd never seen her eat before in his apartment.

"Stop!" Melody dropped her fork. "We have to say grace."

Her shoulders sagged and she rolled her eyes, continuing to chew and swallow. "Really, Jones? Grace? Since when do you give reverence to the Lord for anything?"

"I actually go to church every Sunday." He wasn't lying. His mother always threatened to come back and haunt him if he didn't go to church and pray. He remembered something from the Bible. *Raise up the child....*

"Really?" She had her eyebrow perched high again.

"You don't believe me? I thought we agreed yesterday that I would be honest with you. Now, you don't believe a word I'm saying."

"Prove it." Her eyebrow dropped slightly, but he could tell her expression was softening. *Okay, fine.*

"I'm true to this, not new to this." She started giggling. "Give me your hands."

With her hands in his, he began. "We give thanks to you, Lord, for this food that we are about to receive, and we pray that it will give nourishment to our bodies so that we may better serve you, in your son Jesus' name. Amen." He squeezed her hand slightly, the way his mother used to, and he opened his eyes. When he looked up, Melody was already staring at him. He didn't bother trying to read her expression.

"What did I not do now?"

"I didn't know you grew up in the church."

"Well, you never really had time to ask."

She huffed at him and rolled her eyes. He looked at her and examined her features. The bow of her nose was thin, and her nostrils were small; she had high cheekbones and full lips. Her eyes were a version of dark hazel that he'd never seen before. There were definite traces of another culture in her features, but the prevailing, undeniable truth was that she was of African descent. Her hair was long and thick, but it curled tightly when it was wet. Her skin tanned the hotter the sun blazed in summer, and her teeth gleamed whiter. The only thing that did not change was her eyes.

"Quit staring at me. You're making me feel creepy. You'd better have a good reason for waking me up, too."

"Of course I do. Eat up."

The church parking lot was packed. Several of Jones' employees that attended the church including his secretary Danielle were attending the wedding. After spotting Danielle, Jones walked over to her and began whispering hurriedly. Melody didn't claim to be the type to be jealous, but Jones recognized the green in her scowl when he turned around.

"Melody, this is my secretary Danielle."

Danielle extended her hand to shake and murmured a polite "Nice to meet you" before Melody reluctantly extended her hand and returned the gesture.

"You're going to go with Danielle for about an hour, and she will bring you back to the house, okay?"

Melody gasped and immediately went into a rant. "Jones, I don't know this woman, and you're just going to pass me off to her as if I need babysitting? Where are you going that's so important?" She had seemingly no regard for Danielle's thoughts on the subject or her hand, which she was crushing as her voice escalated.

"Honey, I think Danielle needs that hand if she wants to come back to work."

Melody looked down, and after realizing what she was doing, she began to apologize profusely to the woman who was almost in tears looking at her hurt hand. "It's okay," she whispered, weakly. "I will be okay. I understand."

"Jones, I don't think it would be a good idea to go with her," Melody said, regaining her composure.

"You don't have a choice," he grinned. Before she could object, he turned on his heel and ran to his car. He had to get to his office before they did to organize everything; he only had about forty-five minutes. Danielle was supposed to take Melody back to the apartment so that she could change into more comfortable clothes under the pretense of going for a shopping trip. Then, Danielle would drive her back to the office where Jones would be waiting with one of the pilots that tested all of their new planes and a few members of the staff to take Melody up into the air for a brief flight to Dallas. He hoped she wouldn't try to kill Danielle in the process. *I'd better send her a text.*

"Tomorrow is Monday. Are you going to go to work?" Jones asked.

"I don't have much choice. I don't get to play with planes all day like you." Melody was lying on his chest, facing him while he played in her hair. It was the only comfortable position she claimed to be able to find. He knew that it was really because she liked him playing with her hair.

"You could if you wanted to."

"Boy, please. I'd have to work four jobs to play like that."

"Or you could let me take care of you, and you wouldn't have to work at all."

Melody bolted to her knees and moved away from him, sitting upright and staring incredulously down at Jones. Her independence was being threatened.

"What are you saying?"

"I said what I meant, Mel."

He wouldn't let on any further. *She's not ready for this conversation. Give it another day. You've already made more progress in three days than you have in a year.* He was prepared to wait another year if it meant she would say yes, but he knew he wouldn't have to wait that long. He gave himself until Wednesday.

"Jones, what is that? Why are you on your knee?" The gnawing on her thumb had already been replaced with a slack jaw and open mouth that she covered with her hands. There may have been tears welling in her eyes, but he couldn't tell. He dug into his pocket and produced a small black box.

"This is what's going on. You asked me to tell you, so I'm about to tell you."

When she didn't interrupt him, he looked up to make sure that she was still listening. *She is crying.* A quiet Melody Palomar Alessandra Bice was an opportunity worth seizing.

"I asked you out on Friday, and even though you still haven't given me an answer, I've treated you like my girlfriend for the past five days. You've put up with my nonsense and me for more than a year now. I've held out for a long time, and I thought that I'd be better off fooling around with several women instead of committing to one. Fortunately, I've outgrown that. I don't want anybody; I just want you. Miss Bice, can I interest you in becoming Mrs. Jones?"

The proposition tumbled out of his mouth as he opened the box. He'd spent her Monday in the office out shopping for a ring. He had no idea what to do for a wedding ring or what to look for. Anthony would have been able to help him with that type of thing, but he was busy in Louisiana with Felicity trying to organize a wedding and getting to know his future sisters-in-law. Danielle could have helped if she hadn't been granted a week off to get the strength back in her hand and repair the emotional damage incurred from Melody's incessant questioning. Apparently, she was convinced that Danielle was one of Jones' 'lady friends' and that Danielle was to stay as far away from Jones as possible. When Danielle gave her report of their hour together that Sunday, Jones took pity on his assistant. *My woman is a piece of work, and she hasn't even told me if she wants to be my woman yet.*

He realized he was still on his knee waiting for an answer. If Melody was true to form, she'd make him wait a little bit longer. He couldn't tell what she was thinking; it was the first time he'd ever seen her cry.

"Jones, I don't know what to say," she finally choked out. She was smiling, but her brow was furrowed, and she was contemplative. "I had no idea this was coming. How do you expect me to answer you?"

"With a yes or a no." Jones spoke softly and kept eye contact. Under normal circumstances, that kind of comment would have set her off. She was in an altered state. *Melody in tears... I don't think I like this, but I'm going to use what I've got.* This moment boiled down to the most important sales pitch of his life.

"Oh, Jones." She began wiping away tears. "Stand up. You know I don't like this trite stuff." She began to giggle as well.

As he rose to his feet, she pulled him close to her and wrapped her arms around his neck. A stray tear slipped from her eye, and he kissed it lightly. She nervously bit her bottom lip. *What are you thinking? Please say what you're thinking.*

"Are you sure you want to do this? With me?"

"I am sure that I want to do this. I want to do this with you."

She smiled and looked at him. "I want to do it, too."

Thank God. "So, you're saying you'll marry me?" he teased, tickling her belly with his available fingertips. She squirmed and giggled. *The goal is to stop those tears from falling.* As she laughed and struggled to get away, he pulled her closer.

"Yes," she finally sighed. "Yes, Aloysius, I will marry you."

He frowned at the mention of his legal first name and then smiled. *If anyone should be allowed to use it, it may as well be my wife.* They kissed.

"So," she said, returning her arms to his neck after pushing her hair away, "would you like breakfast, Mr. Jones?"

"Well, Mrs. Jones, that's a wonderful offer, but it's almost five at night, and I think steak would be much better right now."

She laughed. "You know what I meant, boy."

"Uh huh, I've got you all caught up and confused, huh?"

"Maybe," she smiled, batting superfluously her eyelashes. She began to plant kisses on his cheeks and nose, intentionally avoiding his mouth.

"You know, I don't think I want food right now." *You're not teasing me and getting away with it, lady.*

"Then, what do you want?" Her voice was deep, and she was almost whispering. *Oh, Mrs. Jones, you don't have to seduce me. You'll never have to stoop that low.*

"I think we can think of something," he said secretively, pulling her arms from around his neck. He turned around, taking her hand in his and pulling gently. He walked toward his room, which would soon be their room, and he turned off the lights.

I'm really about to get married. Holy shit. Okay, I can do this. I want this. Don't I? Fuck. Where is Anthony? Damn it. Where is he?

Answering his psychic call, Anthony rounded the corner of the hotel lobby where Jones was pacing.

"Why aren't you in the ballroom? We were looking for you."

"Anthony, man. You've got to help me." Jones was panicking. He searched the lobby to make sure that no one was listening to them. Dissatisfied, he pushed Anthony out the doors.

"Jones, what on earth are you doing?"

Jones didn't answer. His eyes were darting back and forth in their sockets. He was sweating, and his hands were clammy. When they finally got outside, he swung around to face Anthony.

"Man, I've got cold feet."

"How is that possible? It's July," Anthony joked, clapping him on the shoulder. He chuckled a few moments longer before he realized that he was

218

laughing by himself. "Jones, are you serious? You're really reconsidering?"

"I'm not reconsidering; I'm just nervous. I mean, this is a big deal. How do I know that this is genuine? How do I know that she cares? How do I know I'm not just kidding myself?"

With every word, the small beads of sweat on Jones' forehead made their way down the sides of his face. He was aware of two things; first, he sounded like a woman, and second, there was a concerned stare on the face of his best friend. *Why did we come down here and decide that this weekend would be the perfect one to get married? We don't have to get married with everyone else. Damn it. Damn it.*

"Jones, you're thinking; stop this thinking. What are the vows, man? What are you going to say to your bride? Remember, those are the reasons why you're doing this."

"Okay," he breathed. "Okay, I remember."

"Say them, Jones. Say them aloud so I know you remember."

"Okay." He took a deep breath and began.

"I, Aloysius Isaiah Jones the Third, take you, Melody Palomar Alessandra Bice, to be my wife. I know that you will be my constant friend and critic, my faithful partner and opponent, and my one true love. Today, I give to you, in the presence of God and all the people that would track me down if I did not, my word that I will stay by your side as your husband in sickness and in health, in joy and in sorrow, through the good times and the bad. I promise to love you without reservation, honor and respect you, provide for your needs as best I can, protect you from harm, comfort you, grow with you in mind and spirit, be honest with you, and cherish you for as long as we both shall live."

Parisian nights reminded Jones of his trips to New York; there were lights and people everywhere, and there was so much to see. Melody brought him everywhere she read about when she was younger. She'd done extensive research on Paris as a little girl and thought of it as the most romantic city in the world. When he first proposed Paris for their honeymoon, she let out such an inhuman squeal that it took several moments for him to recognize the sounds emerging from her mouth were words.

"We can go to the Eiffel Tower and we can visit the Louvre and the Impressionist Museum and the Picasso Museum and – Jones, this is going to be amazing!"

He wasn't surprised when Melody conversed with the man at the front desk in fluent French. *This is her passion. I will add this to the list.* As the weeks passed, he added to a list on his phone of all the things Melody loved and hated. He wanted to know her better, but he was proud when he realized he already knew her fairly well. In essence, she was the female version of him.

She played basketball in high school, ran track in college, and followed football like religion. She was incredibly driven and determined to be more than a Chicago native. During high school, she joined her adopted sister in an effort to start a small organization called M.I.S.T., which stood for Making Individuals Strong Together and taught young girls table etiquette and business in the same setting. The young women of the organization learned how to play golf and participated in mandatory group study sessions. Her sister was the program coordinator now and was doing well back home. Infrequently, Melody would fly to Chicago to host a session and teach the young girls how to conduct meetings.

Jones saw the entrepreneurial spirit in her, but it was her commitment to her community that made him acknowledge his own shortcomings. He thought, idly, that a program like M.I.S.T. would have greatly benefited the boys in his neighborhood.

"I never thought about staying in Mississippi. I was always too convinced that it was the one place I should get the hell away from."

Every night of their honeymoon had become a confessional. He poured his heart out to her, and she would listen; she didn't want to talk. "I'm always talking," she'd say. "You'd get the story out of me without asking," she'd laugh. He loved that she wanted to hear him. He loved that she enjoyed his stories and learning about his life. He knew that none of the other girls he messed with would want to hear him out like this.

When he started talking about his mother and father, he found himself in tears. Crying was an unfamiliar sensation for him. He'd never cried out of sorrow, but it was frustration that drove him to leaky eyes or misplaced anger. Now, he had his head in Melody's lap, and he was staring at the ceiling.

"I hated my mother."

"I don't think that's true."

"I promise you that I did. I hated the fact that she couldn't love me. I always felt as if she was trying to make me into someone she could love. She was always comparing me to Anthony or my father, which caused my hating them, too."

She rubbed his head and looked away, absorbing what he was saying and trying to comprehend. He was aware that he was much less complicated in the days when he was able to kick her out. Now, however, they were legally bound, and kicking her out was not an option. Furthermore, he didn't want to lose her.

"Hell, I just figured out that Ant was my real friend the entire time. It was I that thought I had to fake with him. But when my momma died, I just never thought...." His voice trailed off, and he choked. Melody kissed his forehead.

"I never thought that she'd be right. I just thought that she was trying to put me next to the white boy so we could look as if we needed charity. I was so caught up in my theories that I pushed her away. I didn't think that she cared about me because I was so convinced that she only cared about her white people. It's too late now, though." He was crying violently now and had to sit up.

"It's too late to tell her that I'm sorry and that I shouldn't have said the horrible things I did to her. It's too late to say that I was a world of trouble for her and that I shouldn't have made such a big deal of hanging out with Anthony because, if it hadn't been for him, we wouldn't be where we are today. It was her guidance that made me the man I am, and I've never given her the credit she deserved. I'm Jones of James and Jones Flight because she made me into this man. I wouldn't be here without her."

Melody slid over to him and wrapped her arms around his torso. She rested her chin on his shoulder. "It sounded to me as if you gave her a whole bunch of credit just now."

He slowly turned his head to face her. She smiled up at him.

223

"I don't know, Jones. You said you hated your mother, but you just told me so much about what she did for you that you appreciate. I think, when you were younger, you wanted to hate your mother. Our young minds convince us of things and feelings that aren't ours. I know for a fact that when I was a kid, I was resentful of my brother because he was the only child that my parents didn't adopt. I was angry with my birth mother for not loving me and for giving me up. But, I know now that I wouldn't have received the love that I did from the parents that I did know if she hadn't. You didn't have that experience, but you have the same feelings; you were reared by someone who wanted the best for you and did everything in her power to make certain you could achieve your highest goals even if it meant bowing down to someone else. You did love your mother. You weren't angry with her; you were angry with your father and the white people she worked for because they didn't acknowledge all the things she was trying to do. They didn't acknowledge her goal: to make her son a better man than her husband and to rear a boy in the South to be better than every boy in the world."

Jones felt his eyes widen. He was trying to ingest everything that Melody just said. They'd known one another for a year and never had a conversation that made him so sure that he met the perfect person for him. *I don't deserve this woman.* He pulled

224

away from her and took her hand in his, gazing into her eyes. The tears fell slowly from his eyes , and with her free hand, she wiped them away from his face. He held her face in his right hand and caressed her cheek with his thumb.

"Thank you," was all that he could manage. She smiled a dazzling smile and let out a small laugh before leaning in and kissing his forehead.

"You're welcome."

Chapter 26

"Okay, everybody, we need a picture!" Ebony was beside herself with excitement. The three weeks under Mahogany's care and dinner every night at Mahogany and Carl's kitchen table had somewhat improved her figure, but she was still thin. Her hair was growing, retaining its shine, becoming glossier by the day, and the bruises on her body were rapidly healing. Phoebe and her younger siblings had a glow about them, their eyes bright and happy. Maxine and Phoebe were already turning into close cousins. Carl was teaching the boys how to play football and basketball.

The whole family was standing on the corner of Bourbon Street, and Mahogany frowned. "I'd rather not take a picture right here, Ebony. It's not the nicest place for the kids to be."

"Oh, hush, Mahogany. The children don't know where they are. Besides, you won't allow me to take pictures anywhere else!"

"Just let her take it, Mahogany. She'll feel better," Felicity said.

"You two are always on the same side!"

Where Ebony appeared from at the funeral was anyone's guess. She said that someday she would tell everyone exactly where she'd been and why she hadn't answered the phone. She was dressed in black with Phoebe close behind her in a similar black outfit, cradling the baby in a pink blanket. The boys trailed in behind the two of them in gray and black suits. All six of them looked extremely tired and grief ridden even though the boys didn't know precisely about what they were supposed to be upset.

The funeral hadn't started yet, and everyone was waiting in the packed church lobby. John T. Woods had numerous friends and neighbors, and with both Mahogany and Felicity being engaged, the entire neighborhood was glad to see them and celebrate their father's life and their engagements. There were five minutes before the funeral was to start when Ebony and her children walked into the house. Felicity did a double take. Ebony was so incredibly thin, but she was still as stunning as she'd always been. She didn't let her sister's thinness prevent her from squeezing the air from Ebony's lungs and reprimanding her for disappearing for such a long time. Mahogany in the same manner placed her sister in the vice of her arms and her love.

"Where the hell have you been? We've been worried sick!"

"Felicity, watch your language. We're in church. I'm sure Ebony has a damn good reason for being gone so long." Mahogany narrowed her eyes as a dare to the contrary.

Ebony looked over at Phoebe who glanced up nervously, understanding her mother's silent instruction, and then she walked away, pulling the boys behind her.

"It's a bit of a long story," she admitted, finally.

Her past week was an experience, at the very minimum, and one that she would not soon forget.

"Mommy, I'm tired. Are we almost at the hotel?" Gregory was tugging on Ebony's pant legs.

"Yeah, Momma, when are we going back to the hotel? I want to swim in that pool!" Maxine was now begging Mahogany. Phoebe clasped her hands together in a pleading gesture.

"I don't think we're going to get them to play along with us much longer, y'all. They're not like us. They don't play outdoors," Felicity laughed, looking at her sisters.

"I don't remember your playing so much as your wrestling outdoors, Miss Felicity," Ebony joked.

"That's Mrs. James," Felicity corrected, looking back at Anthony who smiled and nodded approvingly.

"Well, I guess we ought to get back to the hotel, then, if there aren't any objections," Mahogany said.

"Melody and I will stay here. We want to uh... go check something out." Jones and Melody were wrapped in one another's arms.

UNFINISHED PROJECTS

"You know," sighing Felicity, "I've only seen one couple look that 'gaga' over one another so early in their relationship." She gave a furtive glance at Ebony, who appeared to be wrapped in her own thoughts.

"Don't fight against that cord, Big. You'll hurt yourself."

Zebedee Biggs was akimbo on the floor. It was odd seeing him this way. He was completely naked and trapped, tied to the stove with rope. If there'd been a camera, Ebony would have taken as many photos as possible, but she didn't need anything in the way of evidence, no matter how entertaining. She remembered the children were in the car waiting to get away. Phoebe was loading the trunk. *Keep it quick.*

"You know, as much as I would like to beat the living shit out of you for all that you've done to me over the last fourteen years," she choked, "I'd only be stooping to your level. Wouldn't I? And, baby, I don't even want to think about being that low."

He looked at her in horror while she let the pistol hang casually at her side. She had the upper hand as he was naked and vulnerable on the floor. This could go any way she wanted it to. He could die right there on the floor if she pointed that pistol his way; all that she had to do was pull the trigger. *How in hell did she get a pistol?*

229

"I'm going to leave this here," she said, placing the gun on the kitchen table. "If you get your nerve back and you want to get out of here, you can fire it. I'm sure one of these nosy and concerned neighbors will call the police or something. They'll be interested. They're always interested in the things that go on in this house."

She stopped to chuckle and pulled out a cigarette. *When did she start smoking?* The nicotine kept her hands from shaking. She needed to be brave in front of him. He couldn't hurt her anymore.

"But, Biggs," she took a drag and held it deep in her lungs, releasing it slowly, "if you try to find me," she knelt down so they were eye to eye, but she stayed an arm's length away, "if you come after me or our children," – she was relishing the moment – "I will kill you."

Ebony was dressed impeccably in heels and tight jeans that hugged the few curves she had. She was wearing a blouse that frilled at the collar and a vest. Her hair was straight as a bone. If she weren't trying to kill him, she would have been turning him on. Ebony Woods was never anything short of beautiful, even when she was beaten and tired.

"I have a little bit of our money in the car. Oh, and don't worry, I bought the car myself. I got it with my money, so don't go accusing me of stealing from you. I don't give a damn about this house," she said, waving her hand dismissively at her surroundings.

These were the terms of their divorce. He was being told what was going to happen.

"And I think I'd like my children to have my name. Phoebe Woods sounds much better than Phoebe Biggs," she sighed. "Besides, she's the one who gave me the idea." She giggled a bit and took another drag. "They don't even like you. Your own kids can't stand you. You think you can get over on everyone with money. Damn, boy." She threw the cigarette down and put it out with her boot.

Biggs extended his leg, trying to catch her foot with his. The tape over his mouth was making it difficult to breathe. Thus far, he'd only managed to let out a few groans. He'd stopped listening to her. He wanted her to take the tape off of his mouth. Ebony lifted her heel and brought it down hard; Biggs yanked his foot away just in time.

"Don't you touch me," she said, her eyes widening. "You've touched me quite enough."

Phoebe rounded the corner of the kitchen doorway and stifled a laugh. Her father looked ridiculous. Ebony quickly threw a kitchen towel over Biggs to cover him.

"Girl, what are you doing in here? You shouldn't look at your daddy like this!"

"I was just coming to tell you that we are all ready to go, Momma," Phoebe whispered. Then, a bit more boldly, "Are you going to leave him there?"

231

There was contempt dripping from her every word. Ebony was taken aback.

"I haven't really thought about it, honey. But I told him we were leaving."

"Oh, okay..." Phoebe's voice trailed off. She was standing next to her mother. They were almost the same height. Phoebe was starting to favor her mother in many ways. The two of them were just as beautiful, Ebony's long dark hair just as luxurious as Phoebe's dirty-blonde hair. Ebony was taking good care of her oldest girl. She always took care of her children.

"I love you, Mom."

All in the party except Jones and Melody returned to the Omni Royal. While Mahogany and Carl ate downstairs and Felicity and Anthony rested in wedded bliss in a hotel suite, Phoebe and Ebony sat up compiling photos from the ceremonies and filling photo albums. Maxine sat on the floor playing with Gregory, Zacharias, and Dennis while Teresa slept. The boys were growing quickly. Zacharias and Dennis' birthdays were quickly approaching, and Ebony didn't know where they were going to end up celebrating.

"I love you too, Phoebe. You okay?"

She looked down adoringly at her daughter and tried to read her mind. Her little girl grew up too fast, and Ebony worried that Phoebe was too much like Mahogany too soon. She wanted to apologize to her daughter for not standing up to Biggs and for not being a stronger example.

"I'm fine. I just wanted to say something," she said as she sat up.

"What is it?" *This is going to be harsh.*

"I just wanted to say that I think you're incredible and that you're the greatest Mom in the world." Ebony felt the tears well in her eyes.

"You think I'm incredible?" Ebony didn't know how to respond to her daughter's simple compliment. She felt that she'd wronged her daughter in so many ways. She wronged all her children by not standing up to Biggs.

"I just want you to know that I don't blame you for Daddy. It wasn't your fault. You didn't do anything wrong. And you left when he tried to hurt Gregory. You didn't hurt us. We don't blame you."

Ebony couldn't believe what she heard. Phoebe was so much more mature than Ebony realized. She managed to care for her brothers and sister, helped them with homework, and did everything that Ebony couldn't do. While she picked up the pieces of her life, Phoebe was learning how to be a woman. Ebony regretted that her children had to see the ugliest side of life and that she had no way to protect them.

"I am so sorry that I didn't protect you. I am so sorry that I didn't take care of you the way that I was supposed to Phoebe."

"But Momma, you did. You did do everything that you were supposed to do. You took care of me; you took care of all of us. We had the best birthdays because of you, and we got to see you happy at Christmas. Some people don't even have their moms. I'd rather have you than no Mom at all."

The tears were streaming now from both of their eyes, tears of shared frustration being released as they cried and spoke freely. Phoebe had her mother's hands wrapped up in hers and refused to let her wipe the tears away. Phoebe wanted to see her mother's face and let her know that everything would be okay. Even though she was young, she knew enough about caring for someone else to make them her better.

"We have to go, Momma. Everybody is waiting in the car." Phoebe looked at her father sprawled out on the floor. She didn't bother to say goodbye because she knew that she didn't mean it. "I will wait for you outside."

"Okay, honey. I will be there soon."

Ebony had smoked three cigarettes and started her fourth. She glared down at her soon to be ex-husband. "You're going to be served papers soon,

Biggs. I got the lawyer to draft them. Congratulations, you get to keep everything."

Biggs looked up at her from the floor, pleadingly.

"I won't be seeing you later. Bye, Biggs. You be good."

"I know I'm fourteen and that you don't think about me as a grown-up, but I pay a lot of attention, Mom. I know much about everything, actually. I know that you think I shouldn't know anything, but I think that this is the best way for me to grow up. This is the way that's right for me."

Ebony was baffled. She was trying to get a handle on what her daughter was saying. How could she think that this was the best way for her to grow up? Even if it was the only way that she knew, Ebony wanted to give her the best. Ebony wanted all of her children to have it better than their parents. Indeed, Phoebe was enlightening her.

"Phoebe, this isn't normal. This isn't the way you should live, angry with your mother and scared of your father."

"But I'm not scared of him anymore, Mommy. It's because of you that I'm not afraid of him. I was never angry with you. I was angry at what he did to you and the fact that I couldn't stop him. You never let us hurt. You always smiled for us."

Ebony's tears went on unceasing, dripping down her face on her and Phoebe's clasped hands. They were closer now than they'd ever been.

"Where's my phone, Phoebe?" She was driving too fast.

"It's right here, Mommy. Aunt Felicity and Aunt Mahogany called you again."

Phoebe had the phone in her hand. The week before, Ebony went to have the bill changed so that she was no longer attached to Biggs'. All calls from the past week were ignored because she was busy planning how to get safely away from Biggs and the house. They were in Shreveport, but they needed to get as far away as quickly as possible. All she knew was that she needed to get to New Orleans and see her father.

"Where are we going, Mom?" Gregory asked from the backseat.

"Is it going to take a long time?" Zacharias whined.

Dennis and Teresa were slipping in and out of naps. They'd been awake the whole night before and fussed at Phoebe when she packed them into the car. Phoebe spent the week preparing for the major trip that she conspired with her mother to take.

"You guys, be quiet. You're being annoying, and you're going to wake up Teresa," pleaded Phoebe.

"It's okay, honey. We're going to be okay. We will be in New Orleans as fast as I can get there, okay?"

Ebony called on her cell phone as many people she could think of in her old neighborhood, but none answered. When they arrived at her father's house, she knew there was something wrong. There was still yellow tape wrapped around the house. She started to get out of the car and inspect the house but thought better of it. *I need to go to the police. They're the ones that will know what's going on.* "We're going to stop somewhere else, kids."

Gregory and Zacharias groaned, and Phoebe glared at them. Dennis and Teresa woke up and threatened to start crying, so Phoebe started cooing softly at her sister and reassuringly rubbing her brother's knee.

By the time she arrived at the station and the police informed her that her father passed and the services were going to be the next day, Ebony almost collapsed. She couldn't afford to be upset after she'd been so strong for her children. Leaving Biggs was the most difficult decision that she'd ever made. She didn't know what she was going to do, but she knew that she had to do it without him. The most important thing in that moment was holding together and taking care of her babies.

"We're going to go stay in a hotel and get ready for tomorrow, okay everybody?" Ebony managed to dry her tears before she returned to the car, and she sounded better than she felt. Only Phoebe could read her mother's face.

"It's grandpa, isn't it?"

Ebony nodded and a tear crawled its way out of her eye.

"Mom, you're the best woman in the world."

Maxine and the boys stopped playing and looked up at the pair of them, linked by their hands on the bed. Zacharias started to rise and go to the bed, but Maxine held him back and placed a finger over her mouth. "Not right now," she whispered.

"You taught me everything I know. We're going to be okay. We're going to be all right because you're the one taking care of us."

Ebony was now openly weeping and pulled her hands out of Phoebe's and wiped her face. If Phoebe had confidence in her, if her children didn't hate her entirely for allowing all that happened to pass, then there was hope. She would be the strong Mother that they deserved and that they already admired and loved. It was going to be hard, but they deserved it. Ebony knew in her heart that at the age of thirty-one, she deserved it, too.

"I love you, baby. You make me so proud."

Phoebe laughed and cried happy tears, reaching out and grabbing her mother. The two of them embraced and wiped the tears from each other's faces. Maxine walked into the room with Dennis in tow and Gregory and Zacharias walking behind her. Ebony reached out and took Dennis from her niece.

"I just wish I knew what we were going to do. What are we going to do?"

"We'll think of something, Momma," Phoebe said, hugging her mother and burying her head into her chest.

"Aunt Ebony," Maxine started, sitting on the edge of the bed next to her aunt and cousin, truly touched by the displays of affection she was witnessing. "I have an idea."

Maxine looked down at the bed where the photo albums were lying, open and waiting to be decorated by Ebony and Phoebe's able and creative hands. She picked up one of them, the wheels in her head turning faster and faster. "What if you did this?"

Ebony and Phoebe looked up, curious about Maxine's meaning. "What do you mean, honey? You want me to get married?" She giggled playfully. Phoebe's eyes widened, but she laughed, too.

"No, Aunt Ebony, that's not what I meant. I mean, what if you were to plan weddings and parties for people? You don't need anybody to teach you how to do that. You've already planned three weddings this past week. Why wouldn't you do what you love?"

The more Maxine explained, the faster she spoke, and the more excited she became. Of course, Ebony knew that party planning and decorating were the skills in which she excelled. She proved that over the past weekend, purchasing decorations and hiring photographers, establishing an ambiance, and using Carl's kitchen to bake cakes and to cook. It was the one activity that kept her mind clear of everything horrible and the past she sometimes wished she never lived through.

"It's a good idea, Momma," Phoebe chimed in.

Ebony had gleaned so much insight from her daughter over the past fifteen minutes, and all the love from Phoebe – from all of her children – had sustained her through her marriage. Ebony carried on because her children needed her to. She was the same strong woman that her mother was through sickness and in health. When Ebony took her vows, she took them for her children. It wasn't for Biggs, but it was the children for whom she awakened every day. What better affirmation that she could make it over the next hurdle than her daughter's confirmation? Even Gregory was nodding, and Zacharias piped up saying, "Mommy is going to have parties!"

"I don't know how we're going to do that. We have to find out where we are going to live and everything."

"I think I can help with that."

Everyone turned in shock to find Mahogany standing at the door, watery-eyed but smiling. "I asked for a room key downstairs because I was looking for Maxine. I figured she would be up here with her cousins."

"Of course she would," Ebony said playfully, standing and walking over to her sister. She took her hands and pulled her into the room. "I don't think that we can intrude on you and Carl anymore, though, Hog. You two have done so much for us already."

"Oh, hush up, Ebony. Let your big sister take care of you." At this, Mahogany pulled Ebony into her arms and held her tightly to her chest, kissing the top of her head. Ebony's tears began afresh.

"I remember when Momma used to hug us like this and Daddy too would squeeze all of us into his arms. He always fit all of us. Do you remember?"

"I remember, honey. *Shh*. Don't fret about it right now." She rubbed her sister's back and whispered into her ear. "God brought you here, and you're home now. He will take care of you. He brought us all here to take care of one another."

Ebony looked up at Mahogany, smiling through her tears.

"Besides," Mahogany began again, louder than before, "I wasn't talking about you staying at my house."

A broad grin split her face open, and suddenly, the sisters were laughing loudly and playfully hitting at one another. The children all looked at one another, unsure of what was going on between their mothers but sure that some kind of understanding came to pass. Maxine reached over and wiped the tears from Phoebe's face.

"Thanks, cousin Maxi."

"You got it, little one."

"Do you think we are going to be okay?" Her age was showing now, the uncertainty all youth have about the future echoing in every word. Phoebe was happy to be reunited with her family, and she didn't want the love that she felt to go away.

"I know you're going to be okay," reassured Maxine. "Besides," she added, "my momma isn't going to allow any of her little sisters go wanting. You saw how she acted when you all came to granddaddy's funeral."

At the repast, Mahogany pulled Ebony into a corner before anyone could see either one of them get up and leave from the family table or what they were doing. Ebony squirmed in her sister's grip but had an unpleasant reminder of the last time she tried to get away from Mahogany, and she relaxed. Anything her sister was guarding her from or leading her to was for her benefit.

"What are you doing, Mahogany? Jeez, you don't have to pull my arm off."

"Where are you staying and what are you doing for money? How did you get here? You can get past

Felicity without answering her questions, but I hope you knew better than to think that would fly with your big sister. Now, you tell me what's going on here and now, or I will pull you across my knee like a child."

Ebony's eyes were increasingly wider with terror as Mahogany berated her in a low menacing whisper that she mastered when they were younger. She knew that it would be better to answer all of the questions in the order they were asked in order to get away.

"We're at some sleazy hotel. I only have a little bit of money, and we drove here. I was attempting to go to see Daddy, but then we saw the caution tape, so I went to the police. The police told me to come here today." The last piece of information was voluntary because she knew that her sister would eventually ask her.

"What sleazy hotel? How much money do you have? Did you kill Biggs and steal his car?"

"I don't remember the name of the hotel. I only have about two thousand dollars, and no, Biggs is alive. I bought a car from one of our neighbors."

Mahogany still didn't look satisfied but took into account her sister's condition and the fact that the pair of them received a few stares from other people in the church.

"Well, that's okay for now. But you and the kids are coming back to stay with Carl and me tonight, and you will stay there until I say so. Do you understand me, little sister?"

It wasn't a request. Ebony nodded her assent, and feeling defeated, she followed Mahogany back to the table and plopped down next to Phoebe.

"We have to leave after we eat so that we can get over to Aunt Mahogany's house," she whispered. Phoebe looked up and started to object, but she simply nodded and continued to gnaw on a chicken leg.

"Yeah, I remember." Phoebe smiled at the recollection of the food and the stories she heard at the table during the repast. Family was a new sensation and one that she never wanted to lose.

"Maybe you all will move into granddaddy's house," Maxine offered.

Phoebe nodded and didn't think further about it. She was too busy completing her photo album for Aunt Mahogany and Uncle Carl.

Chapter 27

"Mahogany and Carl, your love for each other has transcended time and differences. In the same way that Jesus loves us in spite of our shortcomings or our extra baggage, we stand here today to witness the marriage between a man and woman who have accepted one another in spite of their past in order to live and share their future."

Carl's house was in the same condition his parents left it, and it wasn't because he was nostalgic or yearned for the past; he was too afraid to move anything out of his mother's perfect order. His fear, however, did not stop him from extending a hand to his fiancée. He insisted that Mahogany and Maxine stay with him after it became obvious that Mr. Woods wasn't long for the earth. He knew that it would be better if they were comfortable in a place that looked and felt more like home. After cleaning two rooms for them, prepared to give Mahogany her space, and bringing their things up to his house, he rode back to the hospital to get them. That night he fell asleep alone but awakened with Mahogany in his arms, wrapped around her like a shell. He didn't move; he was created to protect her.

A few days later, at the hospital, Felicity was in Mr. Woods' room, telling her father everything about her life, crying and willing him to stay around a while longer. Mahogany and Maxine were in the waiting room; they'd already said their final goodbyes and didn't want to risk an emotional breakdown. Maxine looked as if she'd aged ten years, her face drawn and ashen from tears. Her mother was leaning on her shoulder, and to a stranger their roles seemed reversed; fourteen-year old Maxine was the one caring for thirty-five-year old Mahogany, who clung to her daughter's middle like a lifeline. Carl felt as if he was intruding.

"I am ready to leave whenever you all..." he started. There was nothing else to say. If they wanted to leave the hospital in that moment, they'd get up and leave with him. If they didn't, he'd sit down next to them and wait until they were ready to go home. When Anthony rounded the corner and sat down next to Maxine and held her hand, it was clear that they'd be there for the duration.

"It is my understanding that the two of you have prepared your own vows. Mahogany will begin."

"Carl, you have been my closest friend for years. You have loved me through thick and thin. You have taken care of my family. You are always watching out for me. Today, I express my gratitude to your parents and to God for making you into this amazing man before me by joining you in marriage. I will love and cherish you; I will hold you when you

246

cry, and I will pick you up when you are down. Nothing will break us because we've been in it too long. To you, I give my all."

Mr. Woods died that evening. Anthony practically carried Felicity back to their car. Mahogany had Carl's hand in a vice grip. When they arrived back at the house, Maxine wasn't in the mood to eat. Carl showed her to her room, but before he could return downstairs, Maxine ran to the threshold and hugged him tightly, impeding his movement.

"Thank you, Carl."

He wasn't prepared for the embrace, but he gladly hugged her back.

"What are you thanking me for?"

"You made my mom smile more the past three days than she ever has. You're going to be a great Dad, too. I can tell."

He was taken aback by the compliment. He thought that Maxine would be uncomfortable calling him Dad. It never occurred to him that Maxine might not know who her father was or that she might welcome a father figure. However, he thought better of questioning either of them at that particular moment.

"You want to call me Dad?"

"May I, please?"

UNFINISHED PROJECTS

"Maxine, you could say 'hey you' and I'd answer." She smiled weakly, and he knew that he'd somewhat lifted her spirits. Her mother was going to be another story. "I'm going to go see about your mom, okay?"

"Okay... Dad."

Maxine turned around before Carl could see her face, and he quietly pushed the door closed. *She's been traumatized, Green. Don't read into it. She might not mean it.*

He shuffled down the stairs and into the kitchen. Mahogany was sitting at the table staring blankly at the wall. Her elbow was propped up on the table, and her head was resting in her hand. If her father hadn't died a few hours earlier, she would have appeared bored. He approached her slowly and moved the chair from one side of the square table so that he could sit next to her. As he sat down, she spoke.

"He thought of everything, you know."

Carl nodded and sunk into his chair, "Yes, your father was a very smart man and always prepared."

"I'm not talking about Daddy."

Carl immediately hushed. *I don't want you thinking about this, Mahogany, not now.*

"He ruined his throat so he couldn't talk about it, broke his fingers so he couldn't write about it, and beat him so he couldn't think about it."

248

She was speaking in an eerie monotone. Carl was scared of what she was thinking and suddenly started pondering about where all his guns were in the house. He couldn't see her left hand or what might be in her lap. *Shit.*

"He made sure we wouldn't ever find out who was responsible. My daddy lay there and got beaten into submission. It is no wonder that he gave up."

"Honey, I don't think you should talk about this."

"Then, what do you suggest we discuss, Carl, the weather?" Her voice was raised, and her eyes were getting wet.

"Mahogany, I'm not saying you can't be upset. I'm just saying that piecing together someone's motive for killing your father is only going to hurt you." He wanted to be brave, to reach out and touch her, but he knew that she needed her space. He wasn't going to interfere unless she wanted him to. When her left hand made its way to the tabletop, he felt his shoulders drop. *Good.* There was a creak on the stairs. *Maxine.*

"I'm so angry, Carl. I keep trying to find a reason not to be angry." She now was waving her Bible in the air. He wasn't even sure where she got it. It occurred to him that she might have been carrying it around with her the whole time.

"The Bible will bring you answers, but you have the right to mourn, Mahogany. Joy comes in the morning, doesn't it?"

She nodded sullenly and hung her head.

"It's only seven," he offered with a smile. "You've got at least ten hours to cry and scream and wail. But don't worry about solving problems right now. Right now, you need to cry."

Mahogany tried hard to smirk at Carl, but it all gave way to body-wrenching tears and heavy sobs. Finally, she reached out to him, and he pulled her onto his lap. She clung to his neck and cried into his shoulder that way for hours. It was the second time he'd ever seen her weak. Mahogany made it her business to be in control of every situation.

It was nine when she fell asleep, her arms limp around his neck. He stood with her legs slung over his arm and walked slowly up the stairs. It took little effort, but when he finally tucked her into her bed, he was satisfied. She began to stir and reach out in her sleep, but he walked out. He took off his clothes and put on a white tank top and soiled boxer briefs. When he finished brushing his teeth and emerged from the restroom, she was standing in the hallway outside his door, waiting for him.

"Carl, please present your vows."

"Mahogany, ever since I met you in second grade, I knew that I would follow you to the ends of the earth if it meant that I got to be in your presence. Of course, I didn't know how to say so, and I ended up showing you. Today, I have the opportunity to prove that I'm willing to give you living evidence of my love for you for the rest of my life. You're still the most beautiful woman in the world to me. I will be here to love and protect you and your daughter as long as I am living. To the two of you, I give my all."

When Ebony arrived, bringing the combined chorus of four small children and a remarkably mature fourteen-year-old conductor, Mahogany made her move into Carl's room a permanent one. There were several rooms in the house so the children didn't have to share, but the youngest of them preferred to sleep with their mother or with Phoebe. As a result, Maxine started to sleep on the couch, falling asleep in the middle of a brilliant sketch or watching a television program. Carl got the idea that he would move things out of his father's old office to make way for the rollaway bed that was in the basement, but Ebony objected.

"We won't be here long. The kids and I can stay in one room. I know Maxi was sleeping in there first."

"Ebony, he has another bed. You all shouldn't be crammed in there like that. Plus, the babies spend all day in car seats," said Mahogany.

"I honestly don't mind."

Mahogany started to impatiently tap her foot, and Ebony crossed her arms. Both had pursed lips, and the storm was brewing. *Ebony isn't a little girl anymore, Mahogany.* Carl knew he was going to have to be a little more forceful about this one. He literally stepped in between them.

"Hey, I've got a great idea." He was standing directly in front of Ebony and looking her directly in the eyes. She was forced to break her staring contest with Mahogany and became sweet the moment she addressed Carl.

"What idea is that?"

It's a long shot, but I have her attention. It might work if I talk really, really fast....

"At the end of the hall is a nursery. I'm sure I could get Anthony over here, and between the two of us and a few screwdrivers, we could set up the crib again, move it in here, and Teresa could sleep in it. There's an extra mattress on your bed, so if you don't want me to take the bed from the basement, at least let me dress the mattress in fresh sheets, and the kids can sleep with you in the bed. How is that?"

Ebony looked overwhelmed, and he heard Mahogany scoff.

"Uh, I think.... Yeah, that will work," Ebony mumbled. She dropped her arms from in front of her and looked as though she had a headache. *Yet another obstacle is avoided; go Carl!*

"Great. I will go call Anthony."

Carl turned around to walk away from the room and immediately ran into Mahogany, who had a deep scowl etched in her face.

"You can't give in to her every time she says you shouldn't do anything. She's never been good at letting anyone but Biggs do things for her. If you want to bring the bed up, you should." Every word left her mouth in an even tone, rhythmic and seething.

"Miss Woods," he said, wrapping his hands around her upper arms, "this is still my house, and I'd like to keep the peace in my house. That means making sure that everybody gets what he or she wants. You complained about where the babies were sleeping, and I arrived at a solution. Whether you know it or not, you won, too." He spoke in the same even tone, playfully mocking her. "The only person that loses in this whole thing," he smiled broadly, "is I because I'm the one that has to move everything."

Carl kissed Mahogany on the forehead before abruptly shifting her to the side and walking off to their room in search of his phone.

"How soon can we clear the tape away from my father's house?" Mahogany asked.

Most of the excitement of the trip had stripped their conversations of preambles. It was a straight away conversational style that they'd adopted over the past few weeks.

"I can call and have it taken down now. Why?"

"I want Ebony to have the house."

Carl was stunned. He always assumed that Mahogany would want to keep the house or sell it to someone else. It made sense that Ebony be given the house; she needed it with all of her growing children. He also thought about the fact that it was the place where their father was murdered. *Maybe if we locked that room.*

"Are you sure that's a good idea?"

"Well, Carl, I don't think anyone would want to buy it after what's happened in the house. Ebony needs a place to live, and she'd never use that room. It's just as well that she has the house and a place to start her new life. Interestingly, Maxi just told her that she should start a party planning business."

Mahogany was standing in front of the mirror changing her makeup. She'd walked in with tears in her eyes and streaks down her face. It was an emotional time for everyone. Carl was lying on the bed and desperately wanted her to join him. He had to go back to work the next day to close up a few matters. There was still no trace of Mr. Woods' murderer. A young woman had been battered in the hospital, and he was supposed to see her again. He didn't want to prematurely leave his vacation; his lieutenant promised that he could do this job so that he could enjoy his honeymoon in peace. *I will be in Charleston soon. That's all I need to remember.*

"Well, I will go over tomorrow and take the tape down myself." Mahogany looked up from her makeup. "And I will make sure somebody goes over to clean up everything." She closed the case and furrowed her brow. "And I will make sure that we change the locks and get all the new keys together and bring them back when I leave the office." She walked toward the bed. *Score.*

"Have I ever told you," she was crawling across the bed toward him, "how wonderful," she was dangerously close now, "you are?"

Mahogany pulled his shirt, and Carl leaned into her welcoming lips to kiss her.

"You could always let me know again."

She giggled and right when she swung her leg over to straddle him, she bit his lip.

"Detective, I'm sorry to bother you, but we've got what looks like a suicide at the hospital. It is the same guy we now know unmercifully beat that girl, Jefferson. They think both are tied to Woods; otherwise, we wouldn't be bothering you with it. The guy has been positively identified as Davis, Jonathan."

Carl sprang from his seat and snatched the paperwork from the man's hand. He sprinted to his car. *How could I not see it?* He started his car and sped recklessly out of the lot. *I just went to visit Jasmine. She wouldn't say outright who hit her; we found her in his apartment. Why didn't I put this together?*

"I can't believe this," he muttered aloud.

Carl drove with his lights and siren on all the way to the hospital; his heart was pounding, and he was scared. *Jonathan Davis did this?* It seemed such a far-fetched idea that he let out a nervous laugh to keep from screaming. When he arrived at the hospital, all of the construction workers were huddled together, talking among themselves and pointing. A few were being interrogated when Carl exited his car to flash his badge.

"I swear, we had no idea he was in there."

"We only looked when we saw all that red stuff dripping from the container."

"That's blood, isn't it?"

It was a gruesome scene. All the photos had been taken, and the blood was swabbed, but Jonathan was almost unrecognizable in the bottom of the container. He was covered in discarded wood and splinters. Half of his brain spackled the far wall of the dumpster, there were flies circling his head, and his body's decay was accelerated by the heat and the closed space. In other words, he reeked.

Everyone on the scene stepped back as workers cut off the side of the dumpster to read the letter he'd scratched into the green metal. Carl didn't want to read the whole letter after he glanced and saw Felicity's name almost three times. He wasn't interested in his motives to kill himself, and the newly wedded Felicity wouldn't be either. He stepped into the hospital and requested entry to any space Jonathan might have accessed that morning. A flustered and frightened Nurse Kennedy pointed Carl to the locker room. Carl looked behind him, and several people from his office were already behind him.

When they stepped into the locker room, they hastily photographed the space. They needed a lock cutter to get into Jonathan's particular cubby. Inside, they found the plastic bag full of tools. *He left all the evidence. I guess it wouldn't matter if he planned to blow himself away.*

"I'm confident that the blood on these tools belongs to Mr. John T. Woods," Carl said, sounding resigned and defeated. *Honestly, who else would have been able to carry out a procedure like this? Damn it, Carl. You should have known better.*

The only unsolved matter was the missing cell phone from which Jonathan had sent the photos, but Carl assumed that it was dumped somewhere. Finding the cell phone wasn't necessary – the case was open and shut. Carl slowly returned to his car and drove back to the office without the lights and the siren.

UNFINISHED PROJECTS

I hope you never forget how much I love you, Mahogany.

During his drive back to the office, he decided that he would keep this information to himself until it was impossible to hide the truth. It would be best if no one knew what Jonathan Davis did. He turned in the plastic bag full of surgical instruments covered in his father-in-law's blood. After a lengthy discussion with the lieutenant, he was ensured that all of the details pertaining to the case would remain discreet for as long as possible. He knew that his lieutenant would make sure that the media didn't have access to any information, and therefore, they would have to keep quiet about what went on without anything good to print.

"I just can't believe all of this." He didn't know who he was talking to, but he was more than glad to have the conversation with himself. He was piecing together his day. Driving back now to his wife would make him sick. He stopped at the Woods' house. The tape was already removed, and he saw that the locksmith had stopped by after he checked the mailbox and found new keys. When he opened the door, you'd never have known anything happened at the house.

All of the smashed pictures that could be salvaged had been repaired, and the glass on the floor had been swept clean. When he walked back to the tool room, he found the key taped to the door. He didn't have the nerve to open it, but he knew that it was clean. He twisted the knob to make sure that it was secure. When he was satisfied, he walked back through the house, but something caught his attention, and he stopped. On the table beside the front door was a photo of the entire Woods' family. He'd never seen it before. Felicity couldn't have been more than four, and she was in her father's arms. Mrs. Woods was seated with Ebony in her lap. Mahogany was standing with one hand on her mother's shoulder and another on her father's arm.

They'd always been this way – Felicity clinging to her father, Ebony leaning on her mother's understanding, and Mahogany anchoring all of them single-handedly. It was the way they'd started and the way the Woods family would finish – alone. A tear made its way out of his eye as he left the house, locking the door.

"I don't think Ebony should have this key. The children might find it, and they shouldn't go in that room."

"I agree. Give it to Felicity."

Carl gasped audibly. Mahogany didn't bat an eye when she said it.

"Felicity doesn't need to visit the room where her father was murdered. If you think a new family would freak out about that particular space, how do you think she would handle it?"

Mahogany put her hand on her hip and explained matter-of-factly.

"She'd handle it well. The room is where she went to grieve over Momma. She can go there for Daddy." Carl knew that he wouldn't be able to argue. He wasn't sure what Felicity did when their mother passed; he was too busy focusing on Mahogany. It was a subject he didn't want to delve into, and he knew better than to argue with Mahogany about the house.

"When should I present Ebony and Felicity with the keys?" Carl's voice was reduced to a whisper. *I don't like this but Mahogany knows best.* They were packing up their bags for their brief trip to Charleston with the rest of the family. Maxine would have to enroll in a new school, so they would be returning early. Mahogany also insisted on finding a new job.

"I will do it, honey. I don't know if you would be comfortable. From the look on your face, I know you think already that it's a bad idea." She returned to packing her suitcase.

Damn. "Okay. Here." He tossed the keys over to her. Almost without looking up, she caught them. He smiled.

"Thanks, hubby," she said, sticking out her tongue.

"Yeah, yeah."

That night at dinner, Ebony and Felicity took turns thanking Carl by ambushing him before he could return to his seat from the restroom. They had two very separate reactions.

Ebony bounced up and down and beamed at him. She was outshining the lights in the hall near the restroom and rattling the keys in her hands as if she could unlock the doors to heaven with the metal in her hands. When he finally stepped completely out of the bathroom, she jumped on him and squeezed the air from his neck.

"Ebony... you're... choking... me," he coughed out.

She jumped back, one hand held up in apology and the other covering her mouth to stifle a giggle.

"Thank you so much! Thank you, thank you!" She'd begun to cry. "I thought that you and Hog were going to stay in the house, but you gave it to me! Thank you!" She was almost reduced now to tears, and Carl reached down and scooped her up into a bear hug.

"You're more than welcome, Little One."

When he put her down, he saw the gleam of recognition in her eyes.

"You used to call me that when I was little," she whispered. She was smiling, but her eyes reflected a reminiscent quality. She was remembering a safer time in her past.

He put a hand on her shoulder. "Hey, you're still little," he said playfully. It was enough to bring her back, and she smiled broadly enough to light up the restaurant again.

When Felicity rounded the corner on Carl as he exited the rest room the second time almost two hours later, he felt his heart sink into his stomach. She was looking alternately at the floor and the key. He knew that she probably wouldn't cry but that she'd either whisper like a child or scream at him. He braced himself for both.

"I'm scared to go back in there," she started. He barely heard her. "Mahogany says I should because that's where everything important is. Everything that's important to me is there in that room. It seems as if that's where everything I love goes to die."

Carl remained silent and listened. *I knew we shouldn't have given her that key. Now she's going to feel obligated.* He found himself studying the same imaginary substance on the floor, tracing tile patterns with his foot and nervously shifting his weight. He jammed his hands in his pockets to steady himself.

"I'm glad that you married my sister, you know. She really needs you. We all do." Her eyes were on him, now, sincerity etched into her furrowed brow. Felicity would always take on the look of a very serious child trying to solve the mysteries of the world. He wanted to reach out and hug her, but he thought that she would do the reaching when she was ready.

"Do you remember when I would tease you about liking her when I was little?" Felicity asked. He nodded his response, looking into her eyes, trying to see where she was going. "I guess this key is some kind of cosmic payback for messing with you like that," she said flatly.

"No. No, Felicity, that's not it at all," the words rushing from his mouth before he had time to decide what it was and why she had the key in her hand. *I really wish they would stop sneaking up on me by the bathroom.*

"Then, what is it?" Her voice was still so quiet. She was still six.

"It's an offering." An explanation speedily made its way to his mind. She cocked her head to the side in a questioning gesture. "It's an opportunity." She still didn't understand. *Okay, let's work this out.*

"You used to tease me and say you'd tell your sister that I liked her, and I took that as a threat. If you had told her that I liked her and I had taken advantage of it back then, I wouldn't have had to wait until Sunday to marry her. This is your opportunity to go back home. You can look at that key as a threat or a way to literally open a door to the past that you left behind and that you miss so much." He paused. "I'm probably not making any

263

sense, but I'm not teasing you, Li. I told Mahogany you shouldn't have the key." He nervously rubbed the back of his head.

Felicity offered a weak smile. "You put it kind of funny, but you're right." She nodded and looked anywhere but at his face, absorbing her surroundings. She put the key in her pocket.

"Thanks, Carlos."

He smiled. "I haven't been called that in a while."

"My first Spanish word," she said with a smirk. He laughed and put his arm around her shoulder as they walked back to their table.

"Excuse me, sir, but I think your wife is over there. I'll take mine back," Anthony hollered from the opposite end of the table.

"Oh, I'm so sorry, sir. You know, it's not easy to resist one of these good looking Woods sisters," Carl joked. Felicity covered her face, embarrassed by the antics of her brother-in-law and husband.

Carl liked Anthony and Felicity together. He knew that she was going to be taken care of as long as Anthony was with her. He sat at the head of the table next to Mahogany and looked down the row at his family. *This is a beautiful sight.*

There they all were, brought together again with their new additions, and he couldn't help but swell with pride. In a way, he and Mahogany had resumed their old roles at the head of the table as the mother and father figures, the oldest at the table, providing for their family in every way they could. There was something reassuring about it that Carl never felt as an only child. He'd adopted Ebony and Felicity in his heart when he took an interest in Mahogany. *I wonder if Maxine ever feels lonely.*

"I want to have children, at least two more," he whispered to Mahogany. Her eyes became widespread. He gestured to Maxine who was holding baby Teresa in her arms, cooing at her and grinning. When Teresa didn't require attention, she was playful with her younger cousin Dennis, or Gregory was pulling at her hair. Mahogany nodded her consent.

"I see what you mean, Mr. Green."

"Good, Mrs. Green."

He squeezed her hand, and she squeezed back.

After everyone returned to the hotel and retired to bed to prepare for their early flight to Charleston, Carl relayed the conversations he had with Ebony and Felicity at Mahogany's prompting.

"Felicity didn't cry," he said. There was a hint of disappointment in his voice. "I didn't expect her to. Ebony did, though. I figured she would after what you told me about Biggs. We should probably tell the authorities where he is, by the way." He was busying himself with pulling back the sheets, so he didn't realize that Mahogany was crying until she sniffed.

UNFINISHED PROJECTS

"Mahogany, what's wrong?" Before he finished the inquiry, he was at her side, pulling her down onto the bed. She wasn't sobbing, but he didn't understand why she was sad.

"I am just so thankful to have you. You've always been here for us, and it was selfish of me to leave you. I know I'm here now, and I know that we're always going to be together, but it's just so incredible to me that we are still in the same position we were when we were fifteen. We're still taking care of one another and everyone else. It's never going to change." She sobbed a little and let her shoulders drop. He wrapped an arm around her.

"I made a decision a long time ago that I would always look out for your family, Mahogany. What would make you think that would change?"

She sighed and shrugged her shoulders. "I don't know. Is it going to change?" she asked, nervously looking up at him. "Will you give up on us if you get sick of us?"

"How could I ever?" he asked, offended. "Mahogany, you're my wife. Your sisters are my sisters. I'm not going anywhere, and you can't get rid of me. You've had me since the second grade in your mom's class. The day you sat down in front of me was the day I became indebted to you. I love you. There's nothing that will ever change that."

He wiped the tears from her eyes and kissed her forehead. She was warm the way she always had been. He pulled her in close, and she rested her head on his shoulder.

"It's been such a long month," she sighed.

"I know," he muttered, planting another kiss on her forehead. "We have a long lifetime ahead of us, though." He leaned back to look down at her, and she met his gaze. "Are you up for it?"

Her face broke into smile, and she looked at him through hooded eyes. She began to nod and then raised herself up and said, "Yes. Yes, I am. As long as you're coming with me, I think I can do anything."

"Ditto," he whispered, taking her chin between his thumb and forefinger and planting a gentle kiss on her lips. She smiled, and he kissed her again. They repeated the process so many times that he lost track of how many kisses he'd given her.

By the time they awakened the next morning, they had to scramble to get in and out of the shower. He was glad that Maxine wasn't in the room when Mahogany suggested they shower together. *I am one lucky man.*

While he was buttoning his jeans, he thought about what Felicity said. *"I guess this key is some kind of cosmic payback for messing with you like that."* The phrase kept progressing its way through his mind, and he didn't understand why. It wasn't until they were thousands of feet in the air that the phrase connected. Jonathan used the same phrase in his letter. It was the one sentence Carl managed to read. *"Some part of me killed your father for cosmic payback, Felicity, for your not being able to love me the way I needed."* He wanted to ask Felicity if it was something that she and Jonathan shared as an inside joke, but this would have been inappropriate and raised suspicions. He would have asked Jonathan, but half of his brain was stuck to the inside of a dumpster.

Chapter 28

"Dr. Davis? What are you doing here?"

He rushed passed Nurse Kennedy before she could ask any other questions and declined to respond to her original inquiry. It was early Monday morning, and he was returning his used tools. He'd also decided to return to the hospital because it was the only place that he could think. He needed some time to think.

The past few days were a slurred dream. Jonathan went to his apartment and found Jasmine there – *why is she still here* – and he'd beaten her so badly. Somehow, he thought he could cover his tracks. He injected her with whatever he had left in his bag from his visit to Mr. Woods. Although he'd been very stingy with what he gave Mr. Woods, his cruel intentions outweighing his sympathy, he was generous with Jasmine.

Maybe she won't wake up.

There was a bottle of procaine in the bottom of his bag. He removed it and used one of her needles, watching as the drug filled the barrel. She was sprawled out on the floor, mumbling. *I think I broke her jaw.* He pinched what little fat she had on her stomach, hastily shoved the needle in, and pressed down on the plunger. Her mumbling stopped.

Good. Now I can leave, and I won't have to come back.

He decided he would dump the bag behind Smokey's since that was the only place no one would ever think to look for a bag full of blood. *I'm not going to get away with this, but it won't be because they figure me out.* They'd try to find him since Jasmine was in his apartment. There was no way he'd be able to hide her anywhere. He just knew that he wasn't going to spend his time wrapped up in white in someone's asylum. His mother showed him what that life was like.

Jonathan visited Oceans Behavioral Hospital and the Psychiatric Pavilion of New Orleans. Both institutions informed him that they had no record of a Mrs. Davis. He decided that he would have to pester his cousin Margaret to get his mother's name as it became clear that Davis was his father's name and not hers. It was around the time that his cousin Big Boy was thrown in jail and Margaret was vulnerable. She'd tried very hard to turn Big Boy around, but he insisted on staying on the fast track to nowhere.

"Momma Margaret, I know now isn't the time, but I have a question that I need an answer to. I need you to be honest with me."

Margaret was despondent. She didn't want to talk to anyone and had barely eaten in three days.

UNFINISHED PROJECTS

She spent most of the day praying and muttering to herself and God. No one could tell to whom she was talking. Her husband spent every day appealing to local law enforcement in the morning and getting drunk at night. Jonathan figured they would eventually separate if she didn't come out of her stupor. She was depressed, but he couldn't figure out why. In Jonathan's opinion, Big Boy was a terrible person and got what was coming his way. *A mother's love, I guess.*

"What is it Jonathan?" She was barely moving her mouth.

"I need to know my mother's name."

Jonathan wasn't speaking loudly, but he said enough to snatch Margaret back to life. She was wide-eyed and suddenly coherent. She was blinking hard and looking at him, rank with incredulity.

"You're asking me about her at a time like this? Boy, are you absolutely crazy?"

He stepped back. She was seated at the table in their crowded kitchen, and he realized that if he moved any farther, he'd hit the refrigerator. *If there was ever a time to stand your ground, it's now, Jonathan.*

"I know you're sad about Big Boy right now, and I know you are trying to get him out of jail and everything. But I'm thirteen now, soon to be fourteen, and I deserve to know who my mother is."

"I spent all this time rearing you and this is how you repay me?"

The words stung him. He wasn't being ungrateful, and he knew that she didn't really mean what she was saying. All the years of being treated like a motherless child made him more than curious; he had to know something, and Margaret was the only one that could tell him. He remained silent and stared back at his cousin who was now glaring at him. There was palpable tension building between the two.

"Fine," she said, stonily. She rose from her chair and strode over to a drawer near the kitchen sink. After shuffling through a few scraps of paper, she produced a small, yellowed slip. She stuck her arm out with her palm face up and the paper lying inside.

After all this time and it's been right here in the kitchen. He thought about all the years he'd spent unloading groceries on the very countertop she was standing in front of. He extended his hand to take the withered piece of paper. When their hands touched, she gripped his fingers.

"You know you're not going to like what you see when you see her." Margaret's voice sounded grave, and he was afraid that she might hurt him, but he couldn't pull away. He wasn't leaving that kitchen without that paper.

"Let go of me and give me the paper, Cousin Margaret. This isn't up to you. You have other things to do. Let me go." He tugged back his arm.

Her eyes began to soften and tears welled. Before she could fight them off, she gasped and opened her palm. Jonathan quickly snatched the paper out of her hand and ran from the kitchen to the room he'd shared with Big Boy and two of his other cousins. The rest of the children were outside, but Jonathan sat on the edge of his bed staring at the small piece of paper. He read it a million times.

"I'm not well," she wrote, "and I think I should leave. Take care of my baby. I will have another one soon." His eyes began to fill with tears.

"Call him Jonathan. His daddy's last name is Davis. Just tell him his momma is crazy."

Her impossibly tiny, scrawling handwriting was almost illegible through the tears that now fell freely from his face.

"I love him, but I can't take care of him, Mags." *I've never heard anyone call Momma Margaret that.* "Love this boy for me, please." "Your loving cousin, Lesley Morris." Jonathan wiped away his tears with the back of his hand.

Luckily, there was no one in the locker room. He'd stuffed a plastic bag full of the bloody scalpels, forceps, and clamps some time during the weekend. Most of the blood washed away in the rain the day before, but he knew that it would take sterilization to clear them completely of any residue. He decided that he would stow the instruments in his locker. His head was buzzing like a radio experiencing interference, and he could barely hold straight his head. When he opened his locker, he looked down and noticed a flash of black metal. He'd forgotten that he owned a gun or the fact that it was in his locker at the hospital. *Probably another one of your brilliant ideas.* He rubbed his eyes with the heels of his hands, hoping to clear his thoughts. There was too much going on in his head. *I just want to go to sleep. I need sleep.*

His paranoia over the weekend had not permitted sleep and caused him to be edgy as he ran from place to place. The fact that he was able to walk straight was nothing short of miraculous. *But we don't get miracles anymore, Jonathan. Not after what we've done.* He frowned and slammed shut the locker door. As he slumped to the floor, he covered his eyes.

Jonathan finally ended up at Meridian Psychiatric Hospital in Downsville on the opposite end of Louisiana. *How did my mother end up out here?* His curiosity carried him far along with a gigantic jar of change he'd collected. After he finished counting it all, it amounted to over two hundred dollars. He only needed about fifty for a round-trip bus ticket across the state. Also, he needed to figure out how to get to the hospital from the bus station, but resourceful as he was, he wasn't worried about it after he befriended a woman on the bus.

Felicity was fitful without him. He had disappeared without telling her where he was going, and his cousin Margaret refused to comment. Anticipation built up early that morning; he was concerned about Felicity's wrath upon his return and the results of his trip. The woman on the bus was meeting an uncle of hers and volunteered his services for a few hours.

"I'm sure my Uncle Joe will be more than glad to help you, dear," she winked. She seemed nice enough. Jonathan trusted her since he was going to be the stranger in Downsville. When they arrived, Jenny's statement rang true. Her uncle was a nice man; he drove Jonathan to the hospital and told him that if he needed a ride back to the bus stop, he would try to return in about an hour. After stepping into the hospital and requesting a visit with Lesley Morris, he wished Uncle Joe had been able to come back sooner.

"How old are you, boy?"

The male nurse behind the desk was considerably taller than Jonathan at his age. Jonathan knew better than to lie, so he squared his shoulders and stood as straight as he could.

"I'm thirteen and five eighths, and Lesley Morris is my mother."

The nurse was slightly taken aback. He studied Jonathan for a moment.

"You look like her. But Miss Morris doesn't have any family, and you're too young to visit her by yourself."

Oh no! She looks like me.

"Please, mister, I've never seen her before." Jonathan became passionate; he hadn't traveled all that way to be turned around. He grabbed the counter and almost threw himself behind the desk. He had to see her.

"Son, your best bet is to wait out here until they bring the patients out for breakfast. I might be able to bring you into the cafeteria with them, but you will not be able to visit with her individually."

His hopes temporarily dashed, Jonathan agreed to the terms laid out; seeing her at breakfast was better than not seeing her at all.

He waited twenty minutes in the lobby under the watchful eye of the nurse and several other attendants. The young man who brought himself across state to see his mother intrigued them all. "I wonder if they've even met," they whispered. "It would explain why she's always murmuring to that pillow in her room." Jonathan picked up bits and pieces of what they were saying, but he was determined not to cry. He had to see her for himself.

276

UNFINISHED PROJECTS

He had to know that she wasn't crazy, and he had to attempt to convince her that she'd given him away by mistake.

In reality, that was his true motivation for coming to see her. He didn't care anymore whether she was as black as Big Boy or as white as the Catholic Jesus. He just wanted to know that his mother actually loved him. He wanted to know that his mother wasn't a loon or a psychopath and that she really did love him and could come home. It dawned on him that his real reason for coming out here was a rescue mission.

Right then, the patients began to file through the hallway.

They were lined up like inmates with identification tags on their left wrists. They all looked afraid to move. You could tell who'd been there for a long time; that's why it was so easy to identify his mother. She stood at the back of the line with a nurse standing on both sides and another nurse behind her. Jonathan didn't even notice the nurse walk up beside him, and he was startled when he touched him.

"Yeah, that's her," he said, answering a question Jonathan didn't think he'd asked in a loud manner.

Lesley shuffled past with her eyes glued to the floor.

"Come on, kid," the nurse sighed. Jonathan knew that the nurse could possibly lose his job for what he was about to do, so he made it a point to profusely thank him before they entered the patient cafeteria.

"Can I go sit near her?"

"Hold on, kid. I need to go over first."

The nurse approached the table where another male nurse who'd taken notice of Jonathan marched over and intercepted him.

"He can't be in here," he growled, pointing a thick finger at Jonathan. The nurse began to explain who Jonathan claimed to be, and Lesley's attendant started to regard Jonathan in the same curious manner as everyone else had at the front desk.

Jonathan ignored him and looked past the two of them to his mother. She was picking at her food. She was very thin, her hair was long and curly, and she was fairer than he was. From where he was standing, she looked very pretty. There was a pillow in her lap. She looked up from her food and swung around to stare at him.

"What are you looking at?" she yelled.

Some of the other patients cringed, but the nurses sprang into action. One immediately restrained her hands while another threatened to take the pillow from her lap.

"No! Don't take my baby! Give me back my baby!"

Jonathan's constrained tears found their release as he stepped back from the scene, horrified. The

278

nurse from the front desk doubled back to him and, with little effort, lifted Jonathan and proceeded toward the doors. "Okay, kid. You've seen your mother, but you need to go now." Now, Jonathan began to scream.

"Put me down! That's my mom! Momma! Momma, it's me! It's Jonathan! Jonathan Davis!"

He realized that he probably shouldn't have said his name, but one of Lesley's attendants snapped to attention.

"Jeffrey, put him down."

This fourth nurse walked over to the pair of them. He was even taller than Jeffrey and knelt down so that he was looking up at Jonathan. Lesley stopped screaming and stared wild-eyed at Jonathan, her hair in her face and her hands pinned behind her.

"Your name is Jonathan Davis?"

Jonathan nodded.

"Shit," the nurse mumbled.

"Jon," she gasped. There were now several patients observing the scene with great interests.

She stepped away from her attendants who began to chase her, but the nurse nearest Jonathan called off the pursuit.

"Ernie, Deborah, it's okay. Let her go."

Lesley walked over to Jonathan after Ernie released her hands, and she snatched the pillow from Deborah. She was squeezing it to her chest.

He stood up from the floor and pulled the gun from his locker. He would have to take this outside. If he went behind the dumpsters where they were working on the hospital, no one would hear or notice him. He sneaked out of the hospital as quietly as he could in the direction of the dumpsters and squatted behind one of them. After thinking better of it, he climbed into one. *I belong with the trash. The woman I loved threw me away. My own mother threw me away. I'm worthless.*

"Momma," he whimpered.

They were now face to face. It was like looking into a mirror. The two of them were alike in every way. She was short, but you could tell that, at some point in time, she was not one to be toyed with. He was looking into her face and on the brink of tears. She'd dropped the pillow to her side and wasn't as interested in holding it now.

"Who are you?" Her eyes were wide and uncomprehending. To Jonathan, she appeared scared. The nurses and patients waited with bated breath. There was a woman in the back who was laughing, and there was a man who kept making noises with his mouth. *These people are crazy. Is she this weird?* All the images of the Black Madonna came to mind. He thought of what he wanted his mother to be. In reality, she was nothing like what

280

he wanted or expected, but he realized that he was more than content with the woman in front of him. At least, he was content until she started screaming at him.

"You're not Jonathan! You're a liar! They sent you here to trick me;" she pointed an accusing finger to the nurses surrounding them. "You get away from me and my child." She started to lift the dangling pillow back to her chest.

Then, Jonathan made his mistake. He reached out to grab her arm. There was a flash, and he read her wristband: NAME: Morris, Lesley, AGE: 33, ID: 99981603772. It was a moment before he realized she'd slapped him; he felt the blood rushing to his cheek and his tingling skin. The tears from his eyes, rolling over the stinging skin, soothed the area before he could put his hand on his face.

"Get away from me! Get away from me!"

Somewhere, distant and far off from him, Lesley was screaming. Jeffrey had made his way back over and slung Jonathan over his shoulder. This time, however, Jonathan did not protest. He was silent the entire time the nurses ran over to him and replaced his hand with ice and wiped his tears away with tissue. They handed him a teddy bear with a white shirt on that read, "I visited Meridian Psychiatric Hospital," and it had a lollipop stuck to its hand. After their hurried exchanges, Jeffrey walked Jonathan outside. Forty minutes had passed, and his face wasn't swollen due to the ice. He pulled the lollipop from the bear and removed the t-shirt.

"Is there someone coming to pick you up?"

Jonathan nodded.

"Would you like me to stand out here with you until he arrives here?"

Jonathan shook his head.

"I think I will, just in case."

About five minutes passed before Joe pulled up and beeped his horn. He rolled down the window and waved.

"Hey, there! I'm here to pick Jonathan up." Joe was smiling, and Joe's smile made Jonathan smile. *I'm going home, now.*

"Thank you, Mr. Jeffrey. I appreciated your help today."

Before Jeffrey could respond, Jonathan tossed the shirt behind him and sprinted to Joe's car. *I will never come back to this place.*

"I got this for Jenny, and you can have this lollipop," he extended his hand. *This is how I will pay these people for being sane.*

"Why thank you, Jonathan. That's very nice of you. Did your visit go well?"

"It was perfect. I'm really glad I came." *I will never talk about what happened today.* He was making more and more decisions during the ride to the bus station.

"That's good. I'm sure Jenny will love this bear. How did you know she loved stuffed animals?"

"Just a hunch."

On his ride home on the bus, he continued to think about his day.

Felicity is going to be everything Lesley isn't. She is perfect. I'm going to make sure I do everything for her because she is perfect. Lesley is evil. It was starting to get dark, so it would be late by the time he got home.

I will never think of her again.

"Are you okay, sweetheart?"

"Yes, ma'am," he smiled.

I will never talk about what happened today.

That night, Lesley Morris cried for hours until she managed to find a piece of metal that was broken off of her bedpost. She looked at it curiously and thought about all of the possibilities. There were so very many possibilities for this piece of metal. One little strip had so much potential. She considered it for about twenty minutes before making an executive decision about its usefulness. When her wrist split, she mused that it was very useful, indeed.

The dumpster was hotter than he anticipated but relatively empty. Jonathan picked up a nail that was on the bottom of the bin and began scratching into the side of the dumpster. *I'm sorry I killed him. It was an accident....*What began as an innocent confession quickly became a suicidal note. His hands were shaking, and he struggled to control them. *I have always loved you, Felicity. I never meant to hurt you.* It occurred to him that hiding in the dumpster was foolish. He remembered playing the game of hide and seek with his cousins. What would they say now if they saw him hiding in the dumpster? *Her name was Lesley, and she preferred a pillow to me.* A single tear rolled down his cheek. There were workers talking outside. He'd have to wait until they started moving the machines around before he did anything that was drastic. *She was at Meridian and her ID number was 99981630772.* The first machine groaned to life outside. *Please forgive me.* His hand stopped shaking. *Jonathan Davis.*

He leaned his back against the wall of the dumpster and inhaled. After writing the letter, he realized he'd been holding his breath. The workers were in full effect outside the dumpster. *Now or never.* He pulled the gun from his waist and closed his eyes. His mother appeared before him – his real mother. Was he dreaming? *Jonathan... what have you done? What are you doing?* He was shaking again and began to cry. "You don't get to judge me. Leave me alone." *You're not Jonathan.* "Leave me alone!"

You're not Jonathan. You're a liar.

"I know I'm a liar."

You're a liar. You get away from me and my child.

"I'm a liar."

UNFINISHED PROJECTS

He lifted the gun to his head and pulled the trigger.

Chapter 29

The house was the same, renewed with the sound of children and the smell of good food. It felt as it did almost thirty years ago when Felicity would come home from school, trailing behind her sister and waiting to get a glass of milk with cookies from Mahogany. She wouldn't start her homework without her milk and cookies.

Ebony invited her sister and brother-in-law into the "Woods Family Home" as the sign read outside the house. Felicity's belly was swollen. She was pregnant with twins, but Anthony was the only one that knew whether or not they were boys or girls. All he would divulge was that they were identical in sex. Felicity didn't want to know; she was just happy that it worked this time.

Apparently, the birth control measures that she'd been taking for years had adverse effects on her ovaries. She had lower chances of conceiving than most women. It took several attempts and much prayer, but they were finally blessed, and Felicity knew better than to complain or take her children for granted.

Phoebe rounded the corner, her hair in pigtails. She'd grown up quickly – at fifteen, she was the same height as her mother and almost as thin. They were the same version of beautiful. It was Phoebe that brought the milk and cookies, now. Gregory, twelve, Zacharias, nine, Dennis, six and Teresa, five all trailed behind Phoebe with warm home-baked cookies in their hands. Broad grins were painted on their faces, and their eyes glittered with mischief. They were a beautiful group of children.

Felicity gingerly sat down, her swollen belly denying her legs comfortable access to the underside of the table. Phoebe brought in the milk and cookies and began to set the plate down on the table when Felicity took it and instead rested it on her stomach. Phoebe and the children burst into a fit of giggles that gave way to uncontrollable laughter. Anthony chuckled, and having taken a seat behind his wife, he reached around her and pulled a cookie from the plate. Felicity pouted at first when the children began laughing at her, but when she looked down at the plate resting high on her belly, she too couldn't help but laugh.

Teresa walked past Phoebe and sat at her aunt's feet, gumming at her cookie. She'd lost her two front teeth and was trying to figure out how to eat the cookie without them. Teresa's preferred seating set Dennis into a fit.

"I want to sit with Aunt Licity!" He stomped his foot down as hard as he could.

If she weren't huge, they both would have been in her lap. She was trying to think of a diplomatic solution when Teresa shifted and sat on her foot.

Just past her belly, Felicity saw Teresa smile up at her.

"Look, Dennis. Reese-y moved over. Come sit on Aunt Licity's foot," she purred sweetly. She nodded at Phoebe.

"Yeah, Dennis. Go share with Reese-y," Phoebe encouraged.

After a few moments of pouting and consideration, Dennis gave in and sat down next to Teresa on Felicity's other foot. Teresa planted a kiss on her brother's cheek and smiled. Even though she was five years old, Teresa still hadn't made the decision to speak. It didn't worry anyone because she used nonverbal communication to explain what she wanted. Her silent nods and finger pointing were all that her siblings and mother needed to reassure them that everything was okay.

"What's up, Momma?"

Ebony re-emerged in a floor length sundress. She was barefoot, and Felicity could see perfectly manicured toes sticking out from under the fabric. There was a broad grin planted on her face. *She's enjoying this!*

"Don't make fun of me, Ebony. This is scary!"

Ebony released a laugh and sat down opposite her sister. Phoebe sent Gregory and Zacharias to watch television and sat next to her mother. Their likenesses were uncanny; both sat with their elbows on the table, their feet swinging under the seat, and

288

both with open-mouthed smiles. *They're adorable together.*

"I'm just happy it finally worked, baby sister. You're seven months along already! It will be eight soon, right?" Ebony reached out and took Felicity's hand in hers, squeezing it gently. Felicity smiled and nodded. "I'm so excited and nervous, but I think that's allowed, right?" Anthony reached out and rubbed her shoulders.

"Of course, you're allowed to be nervous. These are your first children," reassured Ebony, giving Felicity's hand another squeeze. "I was petrified with Phoebe. Worrying about anything other than your baby is unnatural, Li. That's what being a mom means."

Felicity sighed. Anthony interjected.

"You know, the babies are due on Li's birthday." He was beaming with pride. He was excited to be a father; he'd made a list of names and was already looking at houses in River Oaks. Barry and Mitch were going to come down and help him put together the furniture in the house while he drove Felicity around the neighborhood and then – surprise – she'd see their new home for the first time. He was more excited about it than Barry and Mitch, of course, but everyone knew that it would be a sweet surprise.

Ebony squealed with delight. "Two more June bugs? Li, that's adorable!"

UNFINISHED PROJECTS

Felicity sighed. "Let's just hope they're not as moody as I am."

Ebony and Anthony laughed. Felicity shot Anthony a look, and he immediately stopped laughing, which made Ebony laugh even more hardily.

"You still can't win, Anthony. She's always going to be like this." It was difficult for Ebony to breathe between giggles. Phoebe was blushing.

"No, he can laugh if he wants to. He's not going to be laughing when he's changing these diapers," she said, rolling her eyes and returning her attention to the plate of cookies on her lap. During their conversation, Teresa and Dennis had each taken two cookies from the plate. "Are you two eating Aunt Licity's cookies?" she growled playfully, flexing her feet and lifting them off the floor.

The pair of them giggled and Dennis said, "No! It was Reese's idea!"

Everyone laughed. Felicity picked at the two cookies left and pouted at Ebony. Ebony sighed heavily and groaned, "You're such a big baby! Get your own cookies."

"I can't. Your kids are on my feet," Felicity said, smirking.

"Dennis, Teresa, get up so your aunt can go into the kitchen and get her snack," Ebony commanded.

"I will go get them for you, honey," offered Anthony.

"Oh no you don't! Felicity, get up and get your cookies."

"Yes ma'am," Felicity sighed as her niece and nephew moved from her feet and she struggled to rise from the table. Anthony sprung to his feet to assist her, but she waved him away. "It's okay, honey. I'm going to need your help when it's time to sit back down." She smiled at him, and he returned to his seat. *I think I will take the long way to the kitchen.*

"Where are you going?" Ebony called out.

"I'm going to look in at Greg and Zach. Am I allowed?" Felicity chided.

"Yeah, whatever. I'm going to call Mahogany and Carl over here, and they will put you in order."

Felicity smiled. "Call them. I'd like to see my nephew!"

She moved slowly through the halls and paused by the living room. Gregory and Zacharias were enthralled in cartoons. They'd helped themselves to a plate full of cookies as well, and Felicity watched as they mindlessly stuffed confection after confection into their mouths.

Are all children that easily distracted? They can't even look down at their cookies for fear of missing something on the television. She shook her head and smiled. Then, remembering her own hunt for cookies, she turned the corner to take the hall toward the kitchen. Before she could get there, she

291

stopped in front of another door. It was locked, and she knew there was no one behind it, but she could still hear the familiar sounds of carpentry.

"Now, you have to be very careful with the hammer, Bumblebee. You can smash your fingers if you're not paying attention."

She was six and her father's tutelage was boring at times, but she still watched and listened respectfully. They went through all the easy things first, sanding and polishing, staining, and other forms of finishes. Woodwork was not the ideal activity for a six year old, but Felicity excelled at it. Three months after her mother's death, she was an expert with an awl, knew how to manage a chisel, and had completed several small carvings on her own. John was proud of his daughter's progress with the wood and her progress with her grief.

"Now, Li, if you want, you can help me carve out a decoration in this cabinet door for Mrs. J. across the street. Would you like to do that?" He had a smile in his voice, but it didn't make it to his lips.

"No," she replied flatly. Felicity didn't like Mrs. J. She thought she was too nosey, and she didn't appreciate the way her neighbor looked at her father. "I don't like that woman."

John sighed heavily. He knew better than to argue. Felicity told him time and time again that she didn't like Harriet, but she was too young to understand that Harriet would never try anything 'funny,' as Felicity would put it. "She looks at you, and I don't want her doing anything funny," were her exact words. "You're my daddy and my momma's husband and that's it." It was mostly to avoid one of her uncontrollable tantrums that he avoided the subject. Her tantrums were the main reason they were in his small shop.

"I miss Momma. She wouldn't let you work for that lady if she were here."

John sighed. He wanted to tell his daughter that she was wrong again, that her mother would have helped Harriet with anything, that Harriet called herself Mrs. J. because she was raped by white men when she first moved there, and that she would have been shamed out of town for carrying a baby without a father. He didn't have a way of communicating that to the angry, temper-prone six-year-old standing in front of him. Even at six, she looked very much like him. That was one of the reasons he wanted to fix her problem; he knew that, inadvertently, he'd repair himself.

"Come on, Bumblebee. Let's try the small saw."

"Do you know how much I love you Daddy?"

The question caught him off guard. At least she was smiling now, and the grimace had disappeared from the conversation about Harriet. "No, I don't. Why don't you tell me?"

She giggled. "I love you so much that, when I get big, I'm going to get you brand new stuff, and you're going to have a shiny new room." She was bouncing on her toes, excited about her ideas and pleased with herself. Her excitement was contagious.

"That's a lot of love, Bumblebee," he smiled. He was happy the change of subject lifted her spirits, even if it was temporary.

"I love you, Daddy."

She was grinning broadly, and she had her hands clasped in front of her. He scooped her into a hug.

"I love you, too."

"Li," Ebony's voice rang through the hall. When she stepped out of the kitchen at the opposite end of the hall, she stopped and recognized the moment that Felicity was having at the door. She approached quietly and took the plate from her sister's hands. "I've got it, honey," she whispered, "you can let the plate go."

Without looking at her, Felicity released the plate. She put one hand on the door and the other on the knob. "Do you hear him? He's calling me," she whispered. *"Bumblebee."* Before Ebony could say anything, Felicity proceeded to violently slam on the door and shake the knob.

"Oh shit! Li, stop! STOP!"

Ebony dropped the plate to the floor where it broke to pieces and moved over to her sister to try and pry her from the door. Felicity began screaming; she was in a blind rage.

"Daddy! Are you in there? I'm coming! Don't leave without me!"

"Li! Stop! Li, you crazy girl! Stop it!"

The alarming sounds from the hall made their way around to the front of the house, and one by one all of its members made their way to Felicity. The children stopped and stared, but Phoebe and Ebony tugged at Felicity until Anthony appeared behind her and scooped her off of her feet, whisking her away to the living room. He put her down on the couch where she was still writhing and screaming for her father. He grabbed her face in his hands, trying to hold her still. "Breathe, Felicity. You have to breathe."

Ebony and Phoebe had followed him into the living room and pinned down Felicity's arms and legs, respectively. Phoebe was incredibly calm; her siblings watched the scene from the living room doorway.

"I want my daddy. He was there!"

"Felicity, listen to me. You have to calm down. You have to breathe. Just breathe honey." He turned to Ebony. "Has this ever happened before?"

Ebony shook her head. "No. I have no idea what's going on."

UNFINISHED PROJECTS

Unfinished projects lined the walls. Felicity was twenty and just back from her new apartment in Houston. She'd gotten a job as a secretary, and even though her boss was a joke, she was getting paid well enough to bring her father a gift.

"It's brand spanking new. You can carve on this, and it won't leave a single scratch. The table is even so you won't even need the leveler." She was beaming at him while he ran his fingers along the cold metal. "I will finally have a family heirloom! I can't wait to move the table to my apartment."

"Why would you want that old thing in your apartment?" her father frowned. John was grateful for the new table, but he would rather his daughter spend her money on her own things. "Don't you need to save your money?"

"Daddy, when are you going to learn to take my gifts? You never took anything I tried to give you. Even the things I carved for you, you didn't want."

"That's not true, Bumblebee. I love this table, and I always loved your gifts. I just want you to have something to fall back on in case you need money. You can't save if you're spending," he nodded, peering at her over his glasses.

"Well, I wanted to get this for you. So, it's yours and that's all there is to say about that."

He sighed heavily. "Yes, dear."

She leapt into his arms and squeezed him tightly. "I love you, Daddy."

He squeezed her back. There was a tug in both their hearts. *Don't let go.* "I love you, too, Li."

"Li, come on back to me. Breathe and come back, honey. I need you. You have to come back to me, honey. Just breathe."

She blinked her eyes open and shut, and she finally stilled. When she stopped moving, Ebony ran to the kitchen for a glass of water and some ice. On cue, the children sprang into action, looking for blankets and pillows to make their aunt comfortable. Phoebe petted her aunt's head muttering that everything would be all right.

"Felicity?" he was gazing down at her and rubbing her belly.

What happened? What did I do?

"What's wrong? Why is everybody looking at me as if I'm crazy? And how did I end up on the couch?"

Ebony ran back into the room followed by Gregory and Zacharias, who each had a pillow and blanket in their hands. She felt fine. *Why is everybody crowding around me?*

"You have no idea what just happened?" Anthony's concern aged him twenty years. He was still rubbing her belly. *Oh no! Did I fall?*

"No. What's going on? Did I trip? Are the babies okay?" She sat up, terrified of the possibilities. Panic rises quickly when you're pregnant with twins.

"Breathe, Felicity," he said. He was keeping her calm; gazing into those eyes and holding her face in his hand was the best therapy. Gregory and Zacharias stuck their pillows behind her head, and Phoebe helped them pull a blanket over her. She didn't realize that she was cold until the warmth of the blankets sank in.

The doorbell rang and everyone jumped.

"It's probably Mahogany," Ebony sighed, relieved that nothing more traumatic was happening. She walked to the door with Phoebe close behind her. There was a slight noise in the foyer, and Carl Jr. ripped into the room with a paper airplane in hand. All of the children joined in with his game, running around with him, making buzzing noises, and returning to stuffing their faces with cookies as though nothing happened. Mahogany, Carl, and Maxine came into the room behind Phoebe and Ebony. Without any prompting, Phoebe and Maxine pushed their siblings out of the room.

"Okay, crazies. The grown-ups are talking. Let's go upstairs!" Maxine could make anything sound fun.

"I've got a great idea for a game we could play!" Phoebe always sweetened the deal.

When the children all left, Mahogany rushed over to Felicity and dropped to her knees in front of the couch.

"What's the matter with you? What'd you do? Did you hurt yourself?" The questions were being fired a mile a minute, and it wasn't until Anthony touched Mahogany's shoulder that she stopped and looked. "Are you okay?"

Carl was standing behind Mahogany.

"I'm fine. No one will tell me what I was doing. They just asked me why I didn't remember," she said, rolling her eyes at Anthony.

"Don't insult me when I'm not up there to defend myself," he said with a smile. She gave him a stern glare, narrowing her eyes and then giggled. He sighed with relief. "I'm glad you're back to normal."

"Seriously, Li, you scared all of us. You were screaming at the door to Daddy's work room as if there was somebody in there." Ebony was still rattled.

Carl glared down at Mahogany who involuntarily glanced at him. He did not seem pleased. Mahogany coughed. "Well, Li, I'm glad you're back to normal. Is everything okay?"

"Yes, I think everything is fine," she sighed, shifting her weight. *Shit.* "But I'm pretty sure my water broke."

UNFINISHED PROJECTS

She was twenty-six, and the wood room was unchanged. When she opened the door, the fresh breeze disturbed the dust that already began to settle on the countertops and the ground. There was no one else in the house; everyone went to shop with Ebony and the children for new furniture. Her fingers tipped old hammers and screws; she avoided the mallets. She started to hum a ZZ Top song and realized with a smile that she was thinking about Mississippi; she was thinking about Anthony.

"I guess I just needed to come back, she reasoned with the air. "I thought this would be harder." Her fingers lightly skated across the top of the metal table, and a chill went through her entire body. She heard her family's laughter through the house. *They're back already.*

"I miss you, Daddy."

She turned back around and locked the door.

"I still say you should have told me they were boys," Felicity chided. She was smoothing out the blanket over the sleeping form.

"I would have been lying to you if I had," Anthony whispered as he put his second daughter into the crib next to her sister.

"It's not about that. It's about blue. I think they'd look good in blue." She was rubbing Mina's cheek.

"I like the yellow and green. Everybody would think they were boys if we had them in blue."

UNFINISHED PROJECTS

Anthony bent over the rail and kissed his daughter Maya's forehead.

"That's the problem with the world," Felicity sighed, walking to the closet. It was a habit she picked up, checking the closet and any other space where someone could hide. She was paranoid and could care less. *No one will sneak up on my husband, my babies or me.* She clicked on the baby monitor. Anthony walked toward the door.

"You're crazy, woman." He waited for her in the hall.

"I'm allowed, you know," she said. She peered into the room one more time and then left the door cracked open.

When she sat on the edge of their bed, Anthony massaged her shoulders. She quit her job to take care of the twins, but she was still tense. Everything made her nervous; she would only let them lie around in rooms she'd baby-proofed, and every cough or sneeze signified the plague. All of her efforts were devoted to Mina Elise and Maya Eloise.

These girls were only three months old, but they already favored their father. *I hope that doesn't last.* Mina's eyes were green and Maya's were hazel; it was the only physical difference between them. They had the same dark brown hair and sandalwood skin. They blushed like Anthony but smiled like her. *At least they got my smile.* Mina looked as if she might be prone to having a temper. *Just my luck – a little me.*

"So, how long are you going to make me wait for a boy?" Anthony's voice pulled Felicity from her thoughts, and her shoulders stiffed immediately.

"I'm kidding," he cried as she stuffed a pillow in his face.

"Slow down, mister."

Felicity thought back to the earlier time in the year and her episode before giving birth to the twins. *"Li, come back to me. I need you."* Somewhere in her mind, she wanted to believe that it was her father speaking, but he was gone. There was someone living who needed her just as much, if not more than her deceased father. It was his voice and his promise that brought her back; she just had trouble sourcing what took her to such a dark place to begin with. She could have seriously hurt both of the twins or one of her nieces or nephews the way that she was thrashing around.

Anthony had saved her time and time again from loneliness and from herself. It was time that she learned to stop looking for her superhero when he was lying right beside her, muzzled underneath a pillow. She didn't need any more knights in shining armor when her one and true champion already swept her off her feet.

"Hey, you okay?"

There he goes, saving me from my thoughts again.

"Yeah, I'm fine. I'm just trying to figure out if it's safe to have another baby so soon."

Anthony sat up and wrapped his arms around her, resting his chin on her shoulder. "I'm not exactly in a hurry, Mrs. James. I'll be here until death parts us and then some."

"I know."

Finally, I'm complete.

Chapter 30

"Excuse me. Are you Miss Carter?"

He was incredibly nervous when he first approached her; she had a reputation for being about business. He hadn't anticipated her being gorgeous, too.

She'd been complaining about the leaky windows in her classroom for months during the rainy season, and no one bothered to assess the problem. Finally, someone came to fix the window – *a very handsome someone.*

"Yes, I'm Elaine."

"Oh," he said, fidgeting with his hat in his hand. "I was just trying to make sure that I was in the right room." He began to shuffle on his feet at the back of the classroom. His sentences trailed off at the ends as though he wasn't sure what to say.

I'm going to have to do this myself, I see. She came from around her desk and walked toward the handyman. Extending her hand and offering her signature smile she said, "It's nice to meet you Mr.?"

"Woods," he stuttered. He was blinking hard as though he'd never before seen a smile. "My name is John T. Woods. They called me to fix your windows." He finally took her hand in his. She grasped it firmly and shook twice, but he didn't let go. They stared at one another for a few moments.

"Well, Mr. Woods," she cleared her throat, snatching her hand away and becoming uneasy, "it's this middle window here that leaks the worst. The rest of them are a little shabby, but I can deal with them."

She was gesturing toward the windows, and when she looked back over to him, he snatched his eyes away from his mesmerized gaze to pretend he'd paid attention. She smirked.

"Is that all?" he asked, fiddling once more with his hat.

"Yes," she sighed. *You could fix the cubbies in the back and the bookshelf. Not to mention these chairs and my desk could use some care.* She was appraising the room with disgust, and he followed her eyes to all the damaged goods.

"Well, I will get started here and then," he began to shuffle nervously again, "perhaps I could take you to dinner?"

"Are you asking me or are you telling me, Mr. Woods?" Taken aback, her natural reaction was that inherent to her profession; she sounded so much like a teacher that even she was surprised by her tone. *Get it together, Elaine.*

"I'm uh," he stuttered, "I'm not much for words. You'll have to tell me."

She was surprised with how forward he was. "I suppose you're asking me, then. In that case, I would have to accept or decline."

He looked up shyly at her, hesitating before meeting her gaze. *He's too handsome to be this reserved.*

"I guess you're expecting me to give you an answer even though you haven't asked a question," she pondered aloud, her eyes rolling up to the ceiling. She was swinging her arms back and forth and standing on her toes. He laughed.

"Are you laughing at me, Mr. Woods?" She placed a hand on her hip.

"Yes," he said simply. She couldn't help but laugh with him.

Thus, they began their life together. He fixed her windows and took her out to dinner that same night. They hummed along to "Moody's Mood for Love" in his truck when he was driving her home. She was gorgeous, and he was awkward, the classic match of a beauty and her beast. He'd spent more time fixing and building things than he ever had in the presence of a woman. The same quality that made him shy around women was what made him more attractive to her. She loved the fact that he was better at showing her what he meant than saying it aloud.

He carved things for her, and he repaired damaged cabinets and windows in her classroom for a year before he asked if she would marry him by presenting her with a handmade jewelry box with a ring in the bottom drawer.

"I was into romance," he'd say later. "It was easier for me than words."

She was seven years his junior, twenty-five when he was thirty-two, and it was only a week after her birthday that she gave birth to their first child. She was no good at naming children, but she didn't want her husband to name their daughter after a piece of wood.

"What about Mahogany? That's not all that bad, is it?"

It was a rare thing, a full sentence and request from John T. Woods. She willingly accepted the name as a sign since it was one of his first full communications.

Four years later, she was pregnant once more. This baby had perfectly even skin that was dark like night. Elaine thought about her great- grandmother who was said to have the same kind of complexion. They said that her name was Ebony.

"Whether she's dark or not, that should be her name," John offered, his love for the piano he was helping to construct at the time prevailing all of his other sensibilities. "The ebony keys sound sweeter to me anyway."

"Then, Ebony it is," she smiled.

They thought they were finished having children. Elaine was getting older and sicker. She hadn't been to the doctor yet, but she had inexplicable pains in her breasts and stomach. She feared the worst but didn't say anything about it until she found out she was pregnant a third time five years after Ebony was born.

"We're not going to be able to do this again, John. I don't think we'll have the chance."

"I know." His wife's degeneration had not gone unnoticed, and he tried in vain to make her comfortable. Their daughters were getting older and growing faster than he could manage. One woman overwhelmed him, and now he was caring for three with a fourth on the way. He cradled Elaine in their bed. The baby was kicking and moving around in her womb.

"She sure is happy in there," Elaine smiled and then yawned. *I will be too happy to sleep tonight*.

"Hmm," John murmured, dozing.

She fell asleep in his arms that night and gave birth the next day to a beaming girl.

"Felicity," she said, "because she is so happy to see us."

"And we're happy to see her," John smiled.

Just moments before, the doctor told Elaine she had breast cancer.

Epilogue

My name is John. Yes, my name is John T. Woods. I am nearly seventy-two years old. My wife was Elaine Carter. She died from cancer when our baby girl was.... My wife and I have three children. There are only the three of them, three beautiful girls with wild hair and skin like... skin like mahogany and skin like ebony. Mahogany and Ebony... those are the names of my oldest girls. I have one other girl, one last child that my wife and I knew would bring us happiness because of the way she squirmed and kicked when she was in her mother's womb. My baby girl's name is Felicity, my moody Felicity with a smile that outshines the Sun. I'm so lost without my baby girl. She's the last bit of happiness my wife could give me before she....

I just finished having drinks with Jonathan Davis. That young man has a troubled mind. When he broke up with Felicity, he came to me... said I should make her love him.... I don't know how he got that way. He always seemed a little unstable, but Felicity too was like a firecracker. Anyone with good sense would know to leave her alone on her bad days. I wonder if she made him that way. No, I think he'd end up like that either way.

Felicity told me that he was coming back home to work at the hospital. She said that he was doing well in school. They were still friends. Jonathan didn't feel the same. I don't think I like the idea of their being in contact. I remember his cousins Big Boy and Margaret. They both said he had problems. Margaret admitted to me that his mother died in an asylum. No, I don't like the idea of being near him either. Maybe I should go home.

"There I go, there I go, there I go, there I go…. Pretty baby, you are the soul who snaps my control...." This was our song....

I am in the hospital. A young man named Carl Green is speaking to me. He is barely visible. I try to open my mouth and say something back, but there is no sound. I don't understand. Why can't I speak? I want to hold something, but my hands are wrapped shut. I can barely feel my fingers. I can only feel a dull pain. My heart is pounding so fast. Carl has run off to get a nurse. Carl... I remember Carl. He loves my daughter Mahogany. They were supposed to get married, but Mahogany was too scared. But then again, if they'd gotten married, Mahogany wouldn't have Maxine. Maxine is such a beautiful girl. They were in Atlanta. Did they move?

I have so many grandchildren thanks to Ebony and that no good Biggs. I have only seen two of them in person. There was Phoebe; I think that was her name... and a baby boy named Gregory. Phoebe was so fair.

310

UNFINISHED PROJECTS

Her hair... she has hair like her father. Where are they? They still live in Louisiana.

Mahogany is here now telling me not to go. I don't know what day it is. I can barely keep my eyes open. Is that Maxine? Oh, she's so grown up. She has started to look like her mother. Thank God for that.

Carl is on bended knee as he said he would be. All I can do is nod. My head and my heart – I'm in so much pain. Where is Felicity? I need to see my baby girl.

Felicity is at my side, and there is a white man standing behind her. She is talking to me, and he is wiping tears from her face. She is squeezing his hand. I hear her say that they are going to be married and that she wants me to be there, but I've now seen my baby girl. I can sleep, now. I can finally sleep. I'm coming Elaine. I love you, baby girl. I reach my hand out to her heart. I will be right here.

UNFINISHED PROJECTS